SHADOWS AND WHISPERS

SHADOWS AND

TALES FROM THE OTHER SIDE

WHISPERS

COLLIN McDONALD

COBBLEHILL BOOKS
Dutton   New York

Y
M

Library of Congress Cataloging-in-Publication Data
McDonald, Collin, date
Shadows and whispers : tales from the other side / Collin McDonald.
p.   cm.
Contents: Rumors—The soda machine—The slumber party—The
shooting—Nantucket sleigh ride—The heist—Souvenirs—Dressing up.
ISBN 0-525-65184-5
1. Horror tales, American.   2. Children's stories, American.
[1. Horror stories.   2. Supernatural—Fiction.   3. Short stories.]
I. Title.   PZ7.M4784176Sh   1994   [Fic]—dc20
94-2143   CIP   AC

Published in the United States by Cobblehill Books,
an affiliate of Dutton Children's Books,
a division of Penguin Books USA Inc.
375 Hudson Street, New York, New York 10014

Designed by Mina Greenstein
Printed in the United States of America
First Edition   10 9 8 7 6 5 4 3 2 1

TO KIDS—short, tall, fat, thin, red,
black, white, yellow, and everything
in between—who understand, at a visceral
level, that being a kid is a very special thing,
and who understand, so much better than
adults do, that a bump-in-the-night
isn't always merely a tree branch
hitting the rain gutter.

❏

CONTENTS

RUMORS

■ "Do you like Sousa marches?" Gina's friend, Michelle, leaned forward, close to the clarinet section, and kept her voice to a whisper. Mr. Ferbisch, the band teacher, had told everyone to pause a moment, just before the bell rang, while he worked out a trombone phrase. During the pauses, everyone was supposed to keep quiet. Mr. Ferbisch, a nervous little man with thinning hair and thick glasses, didn't usually yell much at the band members, but he was a fanatic on courtesy and keeping quiet during the pauses.

Gina glanced in Mr. Ferbisch's direction. Before she could answer, the bell screeched, signaling the end of seventh period—the last class of the day. Band members hurried to put away their instruments and get to their lockers to grab books before heading toward the exit doors.

"I'm just sick of marches," Michelle puffed, falling into step with Gina on the sidewalk in front of the school. "I know we're a marching band, but I wish we could do some rock or something once in a while."

"We'd probably sound terrible," Gina said, smiling at her friend.

"Know what else bothers me?" Michelle said, adjusting the straps on her book bag as she walked. "I can't stand Mr. Ferbisch. He gives me the creeps. Especially all the talk about his past. He lives alone and they say he has no friends outside of school, and he always has coffee breath. I'm trying to figure out how to have an excuse not to go on the band trip to Phoenix next weekend."

"I don't know if I believe that junk about his past," said Tracy, the second-chair clarinet player, as she joined them on the sidewalk. "I mean, why would they let him teach?"

Michelle rolled her eyes. "Because it was self-defense, that's why. You think every time somebody kills someone in self-defense they just shut down his life and he can't ever work again? Get real."

Gina looked around to make sure they weren't being overheard. "I heard it *was* self-defense," she said. "A housebreaker or burglar or something. And it was, like, ten years ago. That's not what bothers me."

"Oh, great," said Michelle, her eyes growing wider. "There's more? Now I *know* I'm not going to

Phoenix, whether it's regional band competition or not. What are you talking about?"

Gina hesitated. "Well, it's pretty silly, I guess, but I heard kids talking today about something else, something a lot more recent."

"I heard it, too," hissed Tracy, smiling. "That's *really* bizarre."

"What? Heard what?" Michelle's eyes were intense now. She stopped adjusting the straps on her bag and slung it over her shoulder.

"Well, you remember Jason Ardwell, that sort of fat kid from fourth period?" Gina said, looking around again.

"Yeah. He disappeared last fall . . . Wait a minute. They're saying Mr. Ferbisch . . . ? That's crazy. I mean, that's really crazy. There could have been a million reasons why he disappeared." Gina could tell that Michelle was rolling the whole, crazy, bizarre thought around in her head.

"Okay," Gina said, looking around again. "What about Dean Kubicek? Remember him? That was last fall, too."

"Yeah," said Michelle, "but everybody said he ran away. He had this huge fight with his parents over curfew or something. Some of the kids said Dean is probably just living with his uncle and aunt in South Carolina. And Ardwell's probably living with his dad in Seattle."

"I *know* that's what some kids have said, but others are saying something else. They're saying maybe Mr. Ferbisch and the disappearances are connected."

Michelle stopped in her tracks and stared at Gina. "You know how awful that thought is? You know how scary that is, if it's even remotely true? I mean, we're sitting there in band every day, playing our marches, and maybe we're being led by this awful killer? That's terrible! That's *worse* than terrible."

Gina shrugged. "You wanted to know. I'm just telling you what some of the kids are saying. In fact, I heard that the administration knows about the rumors, and now Mr. Morgan and Mr. Warren are planning on talking to the whole student body over the speaker system tomorrow. My friend Julie's mom works in the office, and that's what she said."

❑ The next morning, after the usual announcements over the room speakers during first period, students in all the rooms heard the principal, Mr. Morgan, clear his throat and begin talking about "certain rumors" that seemed to be spreading through school about one of the faculty members. "Most of you know what I'm talking about," he said. "Rumors, especially vicious ones of this sort, can be cruel and are disruptive to the school. Although they are unfounded, they are likely to persist unless we all agree to stop engaging in this sort of idle gossip." Mr. Morgan had a reputation for being very stern, but he was also known to be fair and kind. Gina could hear the concern in his voice as he spoke.

When Mr. Morgan finished, the voice of the superintendent, Mr. Warren, came over the speaker. Although he, too, was known to be a fair and decent man, he now was clearly upset. "Teaching is a sacred profession," he said. "Your chances of being harmed by a classroom teacher are no greater than being attacked for no reason by the clerk in your neighborhood grocery store, or by your dentist."

❏ "What did you think?" Michelle asked after first period, as she and Gina were walking to gym class.

Gina shrugged. "I don't know, I guess. I think I'd feel better if I could see the school's records on Mr. Ferbisch. You know, what's in his personnel file. I think I'd feel better about things."

"Well," Michelle said, "that should be easy. Just break into the school. After that, you could try robbing a few banks."

Gina scowled. "I'm serious."

"You can't be serious."

"Dead serious. I want you and Tracy to come with me. It isn't that hard to get in on a weekend. We can slip into the office on Saturday morning during gymnastics practice. Sometimes the janitor leaves the doors open."

Michelle stopped and stared at her friend. "You're talking about illegal entry. About going into your own school office. Talk about trouble."

"Not exactly." Gina tried to sound patient. "I'm talking about knowing, once and for all, whether or

5

not we're associating every day with a murderer. Is that worth the risk?"

❏ When the phone in her room rang that evening, Gina was awake, staring at her ceiling. "Anybody who can overhear?" It was Michelle's voice, thin and nervous.

"Of course not. I'm alone in my room, like always."

"We're in. I mean, I talked to Tracy, and we decided we've just got to know."

"Saturday, then," Gina whispered. She hung up the phone, already feeling like some sort of burglar. For the rest of the night, and the following night, too, she was able to sleep only a few minutes at a time. Visions of police and newspaper headlines flashed through her mind. If they were caught, would she be expelled from school? Would she have a police record? On the other hand, what if Mr. Ferbisch *was* some sort of killer? Would they have anything about it in his personnel file?

Probably not. But she had to see it anyway, just to put her mind at ease.

❏ On Saturday morning, she almost fell off the balance beam twice during the first few minutes of gymnastics practice. She could tell that Michelle and Tracy were tired, too, probably for the same reason. When Ms. Durham, the gymnastics coach, asked her what was wrong, she made up a lame excuse about having eaten something that didn't agree with her.

Finally, the team took a break, and Ms. Durham went out to her car to get some schedules for upcoming gymnastic meets. Gina signaled to her two friends and they all left the gym to go to the "bathroom." Once in the hall, they sprinted for the school office. Just as Gina had predicted, the janitor had left the doors open while he cleaned. They checked for any sign of the janitor, then Michelle and Gina went inside the office while Tracy stood guard in the hallway outside.

In seconds, Gina found a file cabinet with PERSONNEL stenciled on the outside. She pulled it open as silently as possible and pawed through dozens of Manila file folders until she reached one marked FERBISCH. Inside were several administrative forms, notes, and letters.

"Well?" Michelle whispered, looking about nervously. "What do you have?"

"Bingo!" Gina yanked one of the letters from the file and turned so she could read it more easily in the dim light. "From the principal at another school," she hissed, scanning the letter. "Here it is. Burglar. Ruled justifiable homicide. No police charges filed." She jammed the letter back into the folder, slid the drawer shut, and sprinted, with Michelle, back into the hallway.

"Well, at least we know," puffed Tracy as they raced back toward the gymnasium.

"I still don't know," Michelle whispered as they reentered the gym. "I just don't know. I mean, how can you shoot someone, whether it's justified or not?"

Before they reached the other gymnasts, Tracy stopped and turned to the other two, whispering so low they could scarcely hear her. "Somebody might have seen us go into the office," she said. "I saw a little movement, down at the other end of the hallway, but I couldn't be sure."

"*Now* you tell us?" Michelle's whisper was like a blown valve.

Gina tried to shush her. "We'll know soon enough," she whispered, trying to sound a lot more brave than she felt. "Just don't admit to anything."

❑ On Monday morning, all three girls' worst fears were confirmed when Mr. Morgan called them together into the principal's office. "One of our custodians thought he spotted three girls in the vicinity of the school office Saturday morning. They were in the hall, but he was quite some distance away and he couldn't be certain about anything more than that," Mr. Morgan said. "Now I've checked with your gymnastics teacher, and it looks as though you three may have been the girls."

Neither Gina nor Michelle made a sound. All

Tracy did was clear her throat. She was clearly nervous, and Gina was afraid she might blurt out everything at any moment.

"Now nothing was found amiss, but the staff did find the personnel file drawer just slightly ajar," Mr. Morgan continued. "I have a good guess what happened. Nothing was disturbed, and there isn't anything that can be proven, but I want you three to know something. If there's even the slightest hint that any of you have gone unescorted into this office at anytime in the future, you'll be expelled. You won't come back to school here. Do you understand?"

All three girls nodded, and stared at the floor.

"Now I've discussed this with Mr. Ferbisch, too, and we both agree that all of this rumor business has to stop. Do you understand?"

Again, all three girls nodded.

❑ "Want to know something?" Michelle said, after Mr. Morgan had sent them out of his office. "Now I'm more worried than ever."

"Why?" said Gina. Her heart was still pumping so hard she imagined it was almost making the front of her sweatshirt jump a little.

"Now Ferbisch knows *we* checked on his records," Michelle whispered. "If he really *is* a killer . . ."

"Looks like he's not a mad killer," Gina interrupted. "He'll probably still be the band teacher when our grandchildren go to school." Secretly, she wondered if Michelle and Tracy believed her. She wasn't certain she believed it herself. And the more she thought of it, the more she agreed with Michelle; she didn't feel like going on the band trip, either.

She needed time to think, and to plan. She hated to go on the band trip now, after Mr. Ferbisch knew she and her friends had been looking for his records. The next morning, while her parents were getting ready for work, she put on her worst face and didn't get out of bed. It took her best acting effort, but she managed to convince them that she was ill and should stay home from school and rest.

After they left for work, she lay back down for a moment, and soon she fell asleep. She was surprised when she awakened to the phone ringing, and saw that it was nearly noon. When she picked up the receiver, she almost fainted. The voice on the other end of the line was that of Mr. Ferbisch.

"Just wanted to check and see how you're getting along," said Mr. Ferbisch, who sounded as though he were trying to be as nice as possible. "And I do hope you'll be well for our band trip. After all, you're our first-chair clarinet."

"I guess I needed some rest," Gina mumbled.

"Well, you rest well, and make sure you're fit for the weekend," said Mr. Ferbisch.

❑ "I guess I'll go on the trip," Gina said the next day to Michelle and Tracy. "After all, he

10

did call up and was real nice on the phone."

"Yeah," Michelle whispered. "Like he's going to go around *announcing* he's a terrible guy, or a killer." She paused, thinking. "But I guess I'll go, too. If I don't, he'll notice I didn't go, and if I do, at least you're going."

"Guess I'll go, too," Tracy whispered.

Just after lunch, as the three friends were entering Mr. Bannerman's room for math, they heard the rattle of the loudspeaker in the corner of the ceiling. Mr. Warren cleared his throat and began to speak as the students quickly sat down at their desks.

"This is your superintendent, Mr. Warren," he said, his voice hesitant and a little strained. "Mr. Ferbisch will be on administrative leave for a short time, and Ms. Hartley will be taking over leadership of the band until his return. All band students, please give Ms. Hartley your full cooperation."

"What the heck does *that* mean?" Michelle said, her eyes wide.

"Maybe not a lot," said Gina, still staring at the ceiling speaker. "Could be they just want to clear up the rumor thing, once and for all."

On the bus trip to Phoenix the following Friday afternoon, the band members scarcely talked of anything other than Mr. Ferbisch and his past. Finally, Ms. Hartley got angry and told them all to remain quiet unless they could discuss other topics.

The hotel was beautiful, with large, sunny rooms

and a nice staff. Gina could hardly wait to dive into the shimmering, kidney-shaped pool. Ms. Hartley made everyone go to bed early, since the band competition began at nine sharp the next morning.

On Saturday, most of the band members were too nervous to eat breakfast, and instead waited in the lobby for the bus that would take them to the auditorium. "We're first on the program," Ms. Hartley said after they boarded. "We'll be doing the Sousa marches you rehearsed with Mr. Ferbisch. I want to show the judges, and the audience, that you are the best band our school ever had."

As the competition began, Gina was concentrating so intently on the music that she all but forgot about Mr. Ferbisch. As the band boomed out "The Stars and Stripes Forever," she was still so intent on the music on the stand in front of her that she didn't even look up until the march was over. When she did, she gasped loud enough for Michelle to hear.

"What?" her friend whispered, trying not to be noticed by Ms. Hartley.

"Second row, center," Gina hissed, riveting her gaze on the music and afraid to look up again. She sensed Michelle jump when she, too, saw him: Mr. Ferbisch, smiling, clapping vigorously, and staring straight at them.

The band hadn't been off the stage five minutes before the word had flashed around. Now every member knew that Mr. Ferbisch had watched their performance.

"So what?" said Ms. Hartley, trying to calm the group back at the hotel. "He *is* your band teacher. I'd be surprised if he hadn't shown up. Apparently all the talk about ignoring those silly rumors didn't sink in at all. You still insist on painting poor Mr. Ferbisch as some sort of bogeyman. I think it's great that he cared enough to be here."

Later, Ms. Hartley announced that she had made arrangements for all of them to return home ahead of schedule. After the announcement, she made it a point to visit every room and talk to the band members. "This rumor thing is out of hand," she told each one, "and I want it stopped. Still, there's no point in staying around when everyone is so upset." Within an hour, they were on a bus heading home.

❏ Several days later, the school held a special parent-teacher meeting, with Mr. Ferbisch as speaker. Gina's mother told her later that at the meeting Mr. Ferbisch reassured the parents and teachers that he had nothing to do with the disappearance of the two boys from school. Some of the parents, including Gina's mother, believed him and began a petition to ask the school to reinstate Mr. Ferbisch as band teacher. Other parents, however, drafted a letter asking the administration to delay reinstatement until the matter could be more thoroughly investigated.

Less than a week later, the school was rocked by another surprise: The school administration issued a brief statement saying that Mr. Ferbisch had resigned, and had taken another job totally unrelated to teaching.

"I'm just relieved it's all over," Michelle said during band practice after school the next day.

"Actually, I am, too," said Gina, raising her hand. "May I go to the bathroom, please?" When Ms. Hartley nodded, she turned to Michelle and whispered, "At least, this one lets you go when you have to."

Walking down the deserted hallway, she realized she still had her clarinet in her hand. She thought about blowing a few notes to hear them echo, just for the heck of it, but then thought better of the idea. She was still thinking about echoes when Mr. Ferbisch stepped from the shadow of a nearby doorway. She opened her mouth, unable even to scream, and began to sprint as fast as she could, toward the school office.

"Wait, please!" Mr. Ferbisch called after her. "I just wanted to reassure you and the other band members that I have no hard feelings!"

She heard his steps on the hard floor for a short distance, after which he must have turned and headed in another direction. Gina continued down the hallway, gripping the clarinet like a club. She was prepared to smash it over Mr. Ferbisch's head if she had to.

Reaching the school office, she noticed two of the secretaries inside, working late. She raced into the reception area, still barely able to speak, and continued directly into Mr. Warren's office.

"What on earth . . . ?" said the superintendent. He had his coat on, and held a briefcase in one hand. "Here. Sit down," he said, setting his briefcase on the desk and guiding Gina to a chair. "What's the problem?"

"Mr. Ferbisch," Gina managed to gasp. "I just saw him in the hallway. He was just there, and then stepped out when I went by. I got scared."

"When will it ever stop?" Mr. Warren mumbled, walking toward the doorway. "You wait here and rest a moment," he said, motioning toward a chair. His normally kind face seemed strained now. "I'll go remind Mr. Ferbisch," he said softly, "that he doesn't work here anymore."

❑ Waiting for Mr. Warren to return, Gina glanced about the office. It was pleasant looking, and filled with dozens of photos of fishing and boating scenes, as well as several civic awards. There was even a small piano in the corner. She wondered idly if Mr. Warren could play. Within a few seconds, he was back.

The strain seemed to have drained away. "Just a misunderstanding," he said, smiling gently. "I'm sure he won't come around again." He paused. "Well, I must be going."

Gina glanced again at the piano as she rose from the chair.

"Like my piano?" Mr. Warren said. He seemed anxious to put her at ease. "It's been around the school forever. I replaced a few of the keys. And I'm building a new one of my own at home, just for fun. It's a hobby, actually. I've worked on it the last few nights. I took several of the bones from Jason and Dean, those two boys who disappeared last fall, and ground them into a powder. I mixed it with an acrylic resin base and formed some of the keys. Took forever to polish them. Finished this morning." He smiled again. "I always wanted to be a musician."

Gina's heart nearly stopped, and she felt the blood draining from her face. Her head snapped around toward the door.

"Just kidding!" Mr. Warren said, laughing. He patted her arm reassuringly. "I'm so sick of the silly rumors, I can't even take them seriously anymore. Here!" He gestured toward the piano. "Come and examine the keys. Plain old wood and plastic. Okay, it was a bad joke. But I'm so sick of this. Look!"

Her heart still racing, Gina stepped slowly to the piano, and saw the wood and plastic layers. So Mr. Warren *was* kidding. Now she was both irritated and relieved at the same time. Her face felt flushed and hot. "Guess I'll go back to practice," she said.

"And enough of the rumors," Mr. Warren said, picking up his briefcase.

They walked together, out into the hallway. The secretaries had left by now, and the hallway was silent and empty. As she hurried into the girls' bathroom, Gina could hear the band practicing in the distance. Minutes later, walking in the direction of the sound, she still felt edgy. Every shadow, every pillar, seemed vaguely threatening. She wished she'd forgotten about going to the bathroom in the first place.

She had nearly reached the door of the band room when she realized with a cold shock that she'd forgotten her clarinet in the superintendent's office. With all his stupid joking and everything else, she must have left it on the chair. If she hurried back, maybe the janitor wouldn't have come through yet and locked everything up.

The last thing she wanted to do right now was go back down that hallway. On the other hand, she'd look pretty silly walking back into practice without her instrument. After a moment, she bit her lip and started back in the direction in which she had just come.

To her relief, the outer and inner office doors were still unlocked, and her clarinet was on the chair where she'd left it. She snatched it from the chair seat and glanced at the door, ready to bolt again down the hallway. As she did so, she froze, sensing suddenly that she was not alone in the office, now bathed in the subdued light of a single lamp. Gripping the instrument, she raised her head slowly, and almost fainted when she saw Mr. Warren kneeling on the floor at the far side of the office, beside a body.

Mr. Warren turned and stared at her without

expression. Gina could tell, even in this light, that the body was that of Mr. Ferbisch.

She screamed then, a piercing, ear-shattering scream that carried with it all of the fears, tensions, and worries of the past weeks. As she turned in panic toward the door, her clarinet struck a small, polished wooden box on Mr. Warren's desk, spilling its contents on the carpet at Gina's feet. Tumbling to the floor were fingernails, pieces of bone, a couple of rings, several teeth, and a couple of half-finished piano keys. She screamed again and sprinted through the open door, into the hallway.

Although she was alternately screaming and crying as she rushed down the hallway in the direction of the band room, Gina heard Mr. Warren call to her from his office door. He sounded remarkably calm, scarcely upset.

"Please wait!" he called, his voice clear and unwavering. "I wanted to show you some of these pieces. It will be such a lovely piano . . ."

THE SODA MACHINE

The first savage snarl of lightning, Joe guessed later, must have come while he was still dreaming. It carried head-splitting thunder that left him semi-awake and saucer-eyed, staring at the window, wondering, in the fog of half-sleep, what the heck had happened. He stared at the clock on his night table. It was a little after six in the morning. Too late to try and get any more rest. While he pondered that thought, more thunder, like a burst artillery shell, nearly raised him off the bed.

"You okay, son?" It was his dad, leaning on the doorframe, his voice a quiet counterpoint to the cloud war outside.

"Yeah. Yeah, I'm fine. Heck of a storm." He flopped back again, his head whooshing softly on the pillow.

"Bad day for a storm." His dad smiled. "But it could let up by game time."

19

Joe nodded. The storm would probably let up soon. They always did. After all, didn't Florida call itself the "Sunshine State"? Besides, storm or no storm, he wouldn't be able to sleep now, anyway. The three words that were rattling around in his brain wouldn't let him. And today, those three words weren't just whispering to him. They were shouting out loud. *Freshman reserve quarterback.*

He was barely out of middle school, but because he was bigger than most of the other kids his age, and because he'd worked so hard at football for so long, he had the faintest, tiniest, cobweb-thin chance that he might get a little playing time today.

Coach Anderson wanted him to suit up for the game. And it wasn't any old game. Only the final game with Jefferson High. Only the most important game of the year, the one that determined whether or not football season was over at Howard Hills. His school.

He shuddered a little to think of it. Based on what happened today, the Howard Hills Hawks either would advance to the conference playoffs in another couple of weeks, or they'd hang it up for another year. And everybody would be there. Mr. Malkerson, the principal, was letting the entire student body out an hour and a half early to attend a pep rally. The starting quarterback, Rick Graham, was going to say a few words. Malkerson probably would, too. And everybody would be at the game—the girl Joe liked

20

in fourth period, all his teachers, even his parents.

He drifted into a half-sleep, refusing to move, until the clock radio went off at 6:30, filling his room with the voices of two early morning disk jockeys trying to top each other with lame jokes about the weather. Butterflies were starting in his stomach as he stumbled into the shower. They got worse as he shuffled downstairs to grab some cereal. His friend, Brady, would be here in a minute to give him a ride to school. He'd heard nervousness gives you more energy. Maybe that was good. He needed all the energy he could get.

"Good luck, dear!" his mother called from the kitchen. "Dad and I will be there to cheer!"

❑ "There's a soda machine next to that old gas station we always pass on the way to school," Joe said, leaning back on the car's headrest. "Swing past there. It's a cruddy-looking machine, but I could use a cherry cola."

"At seven-thirty in the morning?" Brady grinned.

"I need the energy," Joe mumbled, "in case I get to play."

Brady was pretty easygoing. He just nodded and stopped in front of the machine. "Hey!" he said, almost as an afterthought. "Looks like they replaced the old soda machine with a new one."

In contrast to the surrounding buildings, the dispenser was modern and clean-looking. A photo in the lighted front panel showed inviting soda splashing over ice cubes in a crystal glass. It presented a marked contrast to the plain, almost run-down station with its boxes, pieces of junk and oily cans strewn about.

Joe stuffed coins in the slot, punched the buttons, grabbed a frosty can and jumped back into Brady's car, tipping the can as he did so. After the first sip, he stopped, held the can close and read the label. It looked like any other label. Yet it was like nothing he had ever tasted.

"What's the matter?" Brady laughed. "Find a mouse in your cola?"

"Different," Joe mumbled. "Real different." He was beginning to feel a little strange, just from the first sip or two.

"Maybe it's just gone bad," Brady said.

"No, just the opposite. I feel *great!*"

"Probably some secret elixir got into that machine by mistake." Brady waved one hand in the air. "A magic potion. Hard telling what might happen."

Joe felt better than he'd ever felt in his life. He sprinted from Brady's car to his first class. He felt so good, in fact, that he had difficulty concentrating on what the teachers were saying. All through social studies, and then English, and finally math, he didn't hear a single word any of the teachers said. The math teacher, Mr. Doheny, got a little mad at Joe for staring out the window when he was supposed to be concentrating on equations.

The pep rally in the gymnasium was a blur of motion and noise. Joe listened with the other players as students around them roared cheers and chants. He barely heard the speeches. Over and over, he visualized himself getting ready to throw, fingers spread on the ball's laces, little finger just below the fourth lace, middle finger on top. He saw himself bringing the ball back with his right hand, close to his head, then releasing the tilted ball with a quick, easy snap, rotating his wrist in a smooth, counterclockwise rotation, followed by a full follow-through.

In the locker room, adjusting the straps on his shoulder pads, he could feel the adrenaline. Whether it was nervousness or the strange soda, he felt as though he had the energy of ten players.

Midway through the game, he still had the energy, but he could use it only to pound the bench with his fist as he watched his team heading straight down the drain. By the third quarter, the Howard Hills Hawks were in serious trouble, down by two touchdowns and a field goal. Moving back to pass, Rick Graham was sacked by two Jefferson players who were much larger and heavier than he was. When he hit the ground, everyone on the field knew he wouldn't get up right away.

"Dislocated shoulder," Joe heard one of the trainers say as they carried Rick off the field.

"Joe!" It was the coach, red-faced, frustrated, jerking his hand toward the field. This was *it*! His big chance. If he came through, he'd be a hero. If he goofed and lost the game, he'd be the school's biggest all-time jerk.

Still, his energy was strong. Before the end of the third quarter, he had sent the ball like a missile for two touchdowns. His arm felt like it belonged to Superman. Maybe there *was* something to that cola! Midway through the fourth quarter, he completed a third and final touchdown, more than 47 yards, to send the Hawks ahead. At the final whistle, the crowd went insane, and the team carried him off the field on their shoulders. It was the most incredible, fantastic day of his life.

❏ The following morning he was up early, even though it was a Saturday, and ate a huge breakfast. Even now, after the exhilaration of the past night, after the roaring crowd and the coach clapping him on the back and all the rest, he still couldn't shake the notion that the soda had something to do with the outcome of the game. To work off the breakfast, he decided to dust off his ten-speed bike, fill the tires and pedal a couple of miles to the station for another cherry cola. If nothing else, it would be a good test, to see if it affected him in the same way.

On the way back, steering the bike with one hand while he sipped the soda with the other, he was almost home when the air was filled with the sickening screech and shatter of two cars colliding less than a block away. Racing around a corner, he came upon a scene that almost made him lose his breakfast. Under the wreckage of two cars, smashed together in the intersection, was one of the drivers, pinned to the ground, semiconscious and unable to move as a growing pool of gasoline threatened to ignite and incinerate both him and the cars.

Joe jumped from his bike and sprinted to the mangled cars as steam rose around him and more fluids gushed onto the roadway. A growing crowd already was gathering, and several people shouted to stay away from the cars for fear they would explode. In one motion, he reached down, grabbed the frame of one of the cars and raised it a foot or so, screaming as he did so for someone to hurry and pull the driver away, to safety. Several men raced over and pulled the man from under the crushed steel as the sounds of sirens grew to a din and more people rushed with fire extinguishers toward the cars.

In the noise and confusion, Joe found his bike, pushed through the crowd and hurried home. Newspapers the following morning carried stories of a "mystery boy" who had miraculously saved the life of the motorist. Television news reported that a business association had offered a reward if the hero would step forward and identify himself.

Telling his parents he was going to shoot some baskets alone, Joe biked to a city park and sat alone for several minutes. His thirst for more soda was more than strong, twisting and wrenching his gut with its power. Twice, three more times in the next two hours he returned to the machine before retreating to the solitude of the park. Now he had a real problem. Clearly, the soda had made it possible for him to lift the car, and, in fact, to win the football game. But how was he going to tell anyone *that*? Something else bothered him, too. His thirst for soda had become all-consuming, a raging thirst from which he felt almost helpless to escape. He wished he'd never stopped at the machine in the first place, even if it had meant losing the game.

He had to tell someone, before this thing drove him crazy. He didn't want to tell his parents. They wouldn't understand, or they'd assume he had some sort of ominous "problem," for which he needed professional help. This *was* a problem, but it wasn't the same. There was something larger and more strange about all this. He didn't want to tell someone like his school counselor, since the counselor would simply tell Joe's parents. He was left with only one choice.

❏ "What can be so important?" Brady said when Joe answered the doorbell. Brady was still holding the bag of chips on which he'd been munching, watching a game on TV, when Joe called.

"Out back," Joe whispered, looking around. If he was going to talk about this, it had to be in private.

Brady's first reaction was laughter. He stopped

when he saw how serious, and how anguished, his friend was. "Okay, okay," Brady said. "Let's look at it logically. What could make soda have such a powerful effect? Drugs?"

"One of my dad's friends works for a cola company," Joe said. "He's told me how incredibly fast their high-speed equipment runs. It would be extremely hard for somebody to put drugs in the cans at the factory. And this didn't feel like any drug I've read about."

Brady thought a moment. "Well, you know where you are," he said finally.

"What does that mean?"

"I mean, where are you? What city do you live in?"

Joe was getting irritated. "Is this a test? I live in St. Augustine, Florida, same as you. What does that have to do with anything?"

"Well," Brady said, keeping his voice low, "I don't have any other theories, so here's a weird one, but it's the only one I can think of. This city is more than 450 years old. You already know that. And you know it was founded by the Spanish explorer, Juan Ponce de León, several years after he sailed on Christopher Columbus' second voyage to America. When Ponce de León came here, in 1513, he was looking for something. Remember what it was?"

"The Fountain of Youth. But what's that got to do with this?"

Brady smiled. "I don't know. Maybe there's a connection. Remember when we talked about this in history class? He was looking around the Bahamas for a legendary island he'd heard about from the Indians. The island was supposed to have a fountain, or a spring, containing water that could make old people young again. He didn't find the island, but on the same voyage he found a new place. Later he named it Florida. He landed just about where we are now. He looked all the way up and down the Florida coast, on both the Atlantic and the Gulf sides, but couldn't find the fountain."

Now it was Joe's turn to laugh. "You're telling me maybe the soda in a machine by a gas station has something to do with the Fountain of Youth?"

Brady shrugged. "Maybe there really *was* a fountain, and maybe the water they use for the cherry cola comes from that spring, or something. Anyway, you got a better theory?"

"This is insane," Joe said, still laughing. "*Any* theory would be better than that one."

"Tell you what we have to do," Brady said. "We gotta go check out that machine again. Maybe I'll try a can of the stuff."

"Don't." Joe shook his head as he spoke. "There's something I didn't tell you. I'm getting so I can't leave it alone."

Brady stared at his friend. "Tell you the truth," he said. "I think most of this is in your head."

They parked a half block away from the machine so they could watch people going and coming for a while. As they watched, a few people bought sodas and simply walked away. None seemed anxious or driven to buy more.

"Looks awfully normal to me," Brady said, smiling again. "Maybe you were hallucinating, or maybe you got hit on the head once too often in the game." Joe shrugged. "Guess I'll just go home," he said. "I think I'll just lie down for a while and listen to my stereo."

He made it a point to appear as casual as possible until Brady had dropped him off. He didn't want Brady to know it, but he was dying to have another soda. In fact, the urge was so strong he couldn't think of anything else. He tried to resist it, to think of the football game, or girls he liked, or his favorite foods, but it was no use. He had to have another soda. Outside, the air was hot, with humidity hanging like a thick shroud, and all he could think of was a frosty, ice-cold cherry cola.

There was no use fighting it. No one was around to see. He had to get down there. He sprinted from the house, grabbed his bike and pedaled as though he were possessed. In minutes he was in front of the machine again. He noticed his hands were trembling as he stuffed the coins into the slot. Instead of the usual thunk! clunk! of a can falling into the tray, however, his coins were returned. He now noticed that a sign with the word EMPTY was flashing over the cherry cola button.

"No!" he hissed. "Is *everybody* drinking cherry cola from this crummy machine?" He walked in a small circle, punching one fist into the other. It wasn't fair. It just wasn't fair. In frustration, he wheeled around and kicked the machine as hard as he could, rattling all the other cans inside.

"Strike me not!" said a voice from the machine. "I will not suffer abuse!"

Joe froze. Slowly, cautiously, he looked around. No one was near. He checked behind the machine. Same story. Just the machine, with its bright front panel and its picture of ice cubes and soda. And the voice.

"Did you say something to me?" he whispered, feeling a little like an idiot for talking to a machine.

"Indeed," said the machine. "I will not be abused." The voice was rich and full, with traces of a Spanish accent. "Cease your abuse, and I will tell you my story. I am lonely, and it has been far too long since I have talked to anyone."

"Who . . . are you?" Joe whispered.

"I am the spirit of Diego Navarre," said the machine. "Trusted friend and confidant of Juan Ponce de León."

"Ponce de . . . That makes you almost five hundred years old!"

"True," said the voice. "And I feel the weight of the years. I could be a thousand, two thousand years old, the way I feel. I must become free of this place."

"What place?"

"This spot. This very spot. Before there was pavement and the filth and wretchedness of man, there was grass here, and a small spring. Ahh, such a spring . . ."

"Why are you here?"

"I am almost too ashamed to tell. I was cursed. I betrayed my master. I found the spring for which he searched, and I did not tell him. I told no one. I wished to have it for myself. And, alas, I received my wish."

"I don't believe I'm listening to this," Joe whispered.

"My master, Juan Ponce de León, a high-born man, later died of a wound sustained in battle," the voice continued. "He went to his grave never knowing that I, his trusted friend, had kept this great secret, and that I would not die. But there are forces in the universe that keep track of such acts, such treachery. For my deceit, I was placed under a curse."

"A *curse*?" Joe looked around again, but no one was near.

"I would live forever, it is true, but I would not be allowed to leave. I would remain here always, as guardian and watchman, so that the location of this eternal spring might never again be lost to future, and perhaps more worthy, generations. I could never leave, unless . . ."

"Unless what?"

"Unless I find someone to take my place. I am given the opportunity to try, once each century. It is a momentous time, a time when the forces of nature respond to my efforts. You may have noticed the thunder and lightning of late."

"That was you?"

"It was nature, signaling, once again, my time of trial and struggle. In past centuries, my efforts met with no success. However, when the people of the garage placed this new, but really quite ordinary, soda machine on this very spot, it gave me an inspiration. Since the new machine brings more people than the old one did, why not use ancient magic—*through the soda*—to attract suitable candidates for my replacement?"

"Wait a minute." Joe already was backing away from the strange machine. "No way . . ."

"Wait! Please!" The machine's light was flashing off and on again. "Listen to me! Right now, in this life, I can give you strength and power of which you have never dreamed! You can be a hero, a football star, the president, a movie star, anything you wish to be. Achieve every dream you ever had! But you must agree of your own free will. And when you are old . . ."

"I have to take your place."

"Correct. And I shall be free. But surely you will find someone to take *your* place, much sooner than I did. And you need not begin fulfilling your obligation here, on this spot, until your physical life on earth is over—many decades from now. Think about it! Now, while you are here, you can have anything you wish!"

Joe smiled. "What's to keep me," he said, "from enjoying all these things, and then refusing to take your place?"

The voice from the machine was soft now, yet eerily menacing. "Do you wish to be cursed forever, with *no hope* of being free?"

"I guess not."

"Then you have your answer."

Joe stopped inching backward and just stood for a moment, his arms folded, looking at the machine. "This is the craziest thing I've ever heard," he whispered.

"Isn't it worth it, to be starting quarterback?" said the machine, in a tone more soft, more friendly, than before. "Just have another cherry cola. Just one. That should convince you."

Joe scowled. "I thought you were out of cherry cola."

"I'm never out. I just flash that sign sometimes, when I am weary of people." As the voice spoke, a frosty-cold, delicious-looking can of cherry cola dropped into the machine's tray. "Go ahead," said the voice. "Aren't you thirsty, on this hot day?"

"Maybe you have lied to me, and I'll still be trapped forever if I agree," Joe whispered, feeling perspiration running in tiny rivers down his back.

"I, Don Diego Navarre, would never lie," said the machine.

"You just did. Didn't you say you were out of cherry cola when you weren't?"

"Not exactly a lie. More like an adjustment of the truth."

Joe's mouth felt as though it were lined with cotton. He wanted that can of cherry cola more than he'd ever wanted anything in his life. His whole system cried out for it. He found himself wavering, arguing with himself. Maybe if he took just this one . . . No! It could only get worse! But then, it *was* hot, and maybe, after all, he just imagined all this . . . Machines don't talk, do they? What could one cola hurt? The thought of a frosty-cold cola was like a powerful magnet, pulling him toward the machine. And yet . . .

"No!" he screamed. "No! No! No!" Forcing himself away from the inviting photo and the thoughts of cold soda, he ran around to the back of the machine and yanked out the plug. Puffing, sweating, trembling, he ran back around, glancing about as he did so. Spotting a jagged chunk of cement lying nearby, he hurled it through the machine's ice-and-soda picture.

"Hey! Hey, you! What's going on over there?" It was the angry voice of someone in the garage. Now two muscular-looking mechanics were running toward Joe and the machine. Joe grabbed his bike, sprinted beside it for a few yards, then hopped on and pedaled faster than he had ever pedaled. Forcing his legs faster and faster, his muscles burning, he didn't slow down until he reached his own front yard. Throwing the bike down on the grass, he ran up to his bedroom and flopped facedown on his bed while a jumble of thoughts tumbled about in his head.

"I'm going to rest for a while," he called to no one in particular, trying to sound as natural as possible.

No one would ever believe this. He couldn't tell anyone. Maybe he *was* losing control of his mind. And now he'd probably never be a first-string quarterback. His performance in the game was probably just the influence of the soda. It just wasn't fair. Maybe he *should* have taken Diego Navarre up on his bizarre offer. No! What Don Diego was offering was slavery, plain and simple! He tossed and turned, trying not to let the thoughts creep into his consciousness. He wondered what had happened to the machine, and whether the garage men had called the police. Most of all, he wondered what smashing the machine had done to the spirit of Diego Navarre.

❏ After more than an hour, his curiosity was too strong to ignore. He *had* to check the machine again. If nothing else, he wanted to see if people were still buying sodas, and if they were acting strangely when they did.

He pedaled his bike slowly, glancing about in case the garage men or the police were out looking for him. A half block from the station, he stopped and left his bike half-hidden in a hedge, then walked closer and leaned on a tree from which he could see the garage and the machine.

He could scarcely believe his eyes. The machine was exactly as before. There was no sign of damage, and the brightly lit panel still showed inviting soda splashing over ice. As he watched, two children walked to the machine, put in coins and walked away with cans, talking quietly as they walked.

"I don't believe this," Joe muttered. "It just doesn't add up."

"Hey, football star!" Shocked, he whirled around, prepared to run, then saw that it was Brady at the wheel of his car. Seeing the startled look on his friend's face, Brady laughed. "What are you doing hanging around here? Spying on the soda machine? Still think it has little goblins inside?"

"I just . . . I don't know," Joe mumbled, feeling a little foolish.

"Need a ride?"

"Naw. I got my bike."

Brady offered a resounding burp, then laughed and held a can of cherry cola above the steering wheel. "Even though there aren't any little goblins," he said, still laughing, "you *were* right about one thing. This stuff, out of the machine, is the best I ever drank. It's incredible. I can't leave it alone. I swear I must have had four or five cans already today. And I'm on my way back for another . . ."

THE SLUMBER PARTY

The invitation was on fancy, embossed paper and was nestled in a foil-lined envelope. Leave it to Anne, thought Patty. She wouldn't even have a simple slumber party without treating it like a grand ball. Maybe that was her mother's doing, though. Mrs. Strebner, Anne's mother, tried to make everything a major occasion. She probably doesn't even brush her teeth, Patty thought, without making it a big deal.

Anne, too, seemed to have the same flare, the same determination to make certain everyone knew her social position. Anne was okay sometimes. She was bright, and she could be lots of fun. But it wasn't always fun listening to her tell how important her family was, and how her grandfather, Wilfred Strebner, had built several shopping centers and stores in the town, and how the town wouldn't have grown to become the city it was today without him. All that was probably true, but it could be really tiresome listening to it all over again for about the ninety-eighth time.

Anne and her parents lived on a large estate set on several acres, not far from Long Island Sound. Every day, Anne's father, Benton, traveled down from Connecticut an hour and a half to midtown Manhattan, where he was some sort of important attorney.

When she first opened the invitation, Patty was excited at the thought of attending a party the following weekend at Anne's home. Anne had nearly everything a girl could hope to have, right at her fingertips. From a visit there once before, Patty remembered a large, oval swimming pool and adjoining whirlpool, only a few paces from a private tennis court. The broad, rolling lawn was perfect for playing games, and there was always lots of great food around. In the family room of the house was a huge projection TV set and sound system that made watching videos almost like being in a theater.

❏ "I think it's great she's having all of you over," said Mr. Carlson, father of Patty's best friend, Cathy, that evening as they roasted marshmallows over a cooker in the Carlson's backyard. "You have to hand it to that family," he said slowly as he picked bits of marshmallow from the end of a short willow stick. "They don't send Anne away to some distant private school, and they're very active in civic affairs."

"Well, they're rich, Dad," Cathy smiled. "It's easy

to be active in lots of things when you've got the money. And they're not all so great. Anne's mother is terrible. She's never friendly to Anne's friends, and it doesn't always look like she's very nice to Anne herself. I'm sure all she's ever cared about was being rich."

Mr. Carlson scowled. "Well, it would be very easy for that family to withdraw, to be very private, to remain aloof. But Anne's family has helped to make this a better city."

"Right," said Cathy, still smiling. "We've sure heard a lot about building this city up from a little town, haven't we, Patty? We've heard how important Anne's grandfather, Wilfred Strebner, was, and how he built all those buildings, and later how he built the shopping malls and did all that stuff. Surprising they don't have a big statue in the city park downtown."

"Well, they've got the fountain," Cathy's mother said. "That was a gift of the Strebners."

"There you go," Cathy said, nodding at her mother.

"Interesting family history," Mr. Carlson said. "Seems to me there was a writer interested in writing sort of a chronicle of that family line one time. I guess nothing ever came of it."

"What's so interesting?" Cathy laughed. "They built buildings. They got rich. End of story."

"Not that simple," Mr. Carlson said. He laid his

marshmallow stick in the grass and leaned back in his chair. "Do you remember that older building downtown, the one with the fancy scrollwork and the figures sort of formed into the concrete in the corners?"

"Sure," Patty said. "I heard they're going to rip it out and put in a health club."

"Used to be a theater," Mr. Carlson said. "Boy, I can't tell you how many movies I saw in that building." He closed his eyes, remembering and smiling. *"High Noon, Ten Commandments, Blackboard Jungle* . . . A lot of hours. A lot of good memories. I can still smell the popcorn."

"What does that have to do with Anne's family?" Cathy said.

"Well, they own the building," Mr. Carlson said. "Anne's grandfather built it. And long after he built it, before they closed the theater, a young woman died in there."

"What?" Patty and Cathy both said at the same time.

"People used to tell that story a lot, when I was younger," Mr. Carlson said. "She was a projectionist, which means she ran the movie projector in the theater. Pretty, too, I guess. Anyway, one night, after hours, the night janitor came to clean up the place and found the girl, dead, in the projection booth."

"That's awful!" Cathy said. "How did she die?"

Cathy's mother shook her head. "I don't think

you should be telling this," she said to Mr. Carlson.

"Well," he said. "It was in the newspapers at the time. Not much of a secret."

"What was?" asked Cathy.

"Took her own life," Mr. Carlson said softly. "Put a rope around her neck, looped it over a steel beam, and . . . Terrible thing."

"Maybe we should talk about something more cheerful," said Cathy's mother. "Such as, who could go for more ice cream?"

"Did they close the theater?" Cathy asked.

"They were going to reopen the theater," Mr. Carlson said, "but it never happened. They rented out offices in other parts of the building after that, but the theater part stayed closed. The old seats and everything are still there today, or so they say. I guess the Strebners felt very bad that something so awful should happen in one of their buildings. Old Mr. Strebner was a pretty decent old fellow, I guess, and he said he just didn't want a commercial business there anymore."

❑ Patty was helping her dad wash their car two days later when Cathy rushed up on her bicycle. "I just heard the most incredible thing," she puffed, letting the bike fall in the grass. "I talked to Julie and Tina—they're invited to the slumber party, too—and they told me Anne was planning something special. You'll never believe it."

"What?" Patty put down her sponge. "What won't I believe?"

"I guess Anne got this crazy idea. You know how she's always trying to impress people. She pestered her dad until he agreed to let her have the slumber party *in the old theater*! Isn't that the creepiest thing?"

"Are you kidding?" Patty couldn't believe her ears. "I mean, isn't that dangerous, since it's downtown, and it's an old building?"

Cathy laughed. "I think it's creepy, and kind of exciting. I guess Anne is going to take the family projector from home and show some scary movies on the old screen."

Patty felt a chill run across her shoulders. "It's weird," she said, "but it sounds kind of exciting."

❑ On Friday evening, eleven girls and two chaperones stood on the walkway in front of the huge Strebner family home. Anne glanced about to be certain everyone had arrived, then walked up a couple of steps leading to the front door and turned back to the group.

"As most of you know, we have my father's permission to go down to the old theater for our party," she said, "although my mother thinks it isn't a very good idea. I guess you can have a choice. We can all stay here and swim and play games, or we can still go to the old theater and watch creepy movies. I've got loads of snacks all ready to either eat here or take along."

"I'm for the theater," Cathy whispered, poking Patty gently in the side.

As Anne finished speaking, Mrs. Strebner, Anne's mother, opened the front door and stared briefly at the group. She was a tall, athletic-looking woman with dark hair and high, graceful cheekbones. She was dressed in obviously expensive slacks and a beautiful sweater. "If you decide to go downtown, Anne," she said, "the vans can stop by in a few minutes. Do let your father know what you decide." She looked again, unsmiling, at the group before closing the door.

Anne nodded, looked at the door a moment, then turned to her friends. "I guess we will have to decide," she said.

"Mrs. Warmth," whispered Cathy. "No wonder Anne's a jerk sometimes."

"Oh, well," Patty whispered. "This time Anne's trying to be nice. And it still should be fun, either way."

The front door opened again, and a tall, dignified-looking man looked out. He, too, wore what looked like expensive slacks and a sweater. "The chaperones will bring the vans around, if you decide to go downtown," he said. His tone was relaxed and cordial. "Perhaps you should all take a vote. As a matter of fact, Anne, why don't you bring the girls into the family room, and you all can talk it over there."

Patty was impressed, just as on her previous visit, when they trooped across the immense marble floor of the hall and entered the carpeted "family room." It was far larger, she guessed, than most of the rooms in her own house put together. Anne plunked down in the middle of the floor, ignoring the TV, and ripped open a bag of snack chips. Some of the girls joined her on the floor, while others sprawled on several chairs and two sofas, all leather, arranged casually within view of a large projection television set.

Photos on the paneled walls showed Anne's family sailing, skiing, hiking, and shaking hands with various politicians and celebrities. "Don't ask her about the photos," Tina whispered. "I did once, and I spent about an hour listening to stories about the French Alps and the Caribbean and I don't remember where else."

"You could almost play basketball in here," Cathy whispered.

"Isn't that *Bride of Frankenstein*?" said Marie, another of Patty's friends, as she stared at the TV screen on which a quaint old black-and-white movie was playing. "That was made about fifty or sixty years ago!"

"I *loved* that!" said Cathy. "Did you see that one, Patty? It's really old-fashioned, but it's great!"

Some of the other girls twisted in their seats and looked at the screen.

"So," Anne said, munching on chips. "What's it going to be? Stay here or go downtown to the old theater?"

"You're right. We'd better decide," Marie said.

"I wish we could take *Frankenstein* with us," Cathy said, already absorbed in the old movie. A moment later, as a commercial flashed on the screen, she turned to Anne. "Hey, Anne, can I ask you something?" she said, stealing a quick glance at Patty, who scowled and quickly shook her head. "I heard some woman killed herself in that old theater your grandfather built. Was that true?"

Anne seemed neither shocked nor surprised. Putting the chip bag down, she said, "I heard that once, too, and I asked my parents. They said apparently it was true."

"*Really?*" several girls said at once. "Why did she kill herself?" Marie's face brightened as she spoke. She turned from the TV and fixed her gaze on Anne.

"I have no idea," Anne said. "Probably nobody knew. My parents just said she must have been very depressed. They said it was a very sad thing, and my grandfather felt very bad that it happened in his building."

"Do you suppose her spirit still hangs around the old theater?" Marie said.

"I wonder," Cathy said, scowling.

"It *would* be interesting to go down to the old theater," Marie said, as several girls shivered at the thought.

"We've got plenty of time," Anne said. "Let's break open some more snacks, and then if we decide to go downtown, the chaperones can take us."

❑ From the outside, the old theater building looked like any other vacant, nondescript building, except for the scrollwork and the concrete decorative figures high in the corners, barely visible in the night shadows. The chaperones, both pleasant-looking, gray-haired women, pulled the two vans around and parked at the curb. From the back of one van, one of the women removed a large coil of electrical cord and a portable movie projector.

"Our chaperones are Margaret and Beth," Anne said as she led the way to the large, locked entry doors below the ancient, paint-flecked marquee. "They work for my father."

The woman carrying the cord produced a key, and after some tugging, managed to pull open the groaning doors. "The entrance to the building's offices, the ones that were rented out until recently, are down the street a little ways," Anne said, as the group entered the darkened lobby. "This theater part hasn't had anybody in it for years."

"Great!" Marie whispered. "Good place for ghosts!"

"Marie!" Patty hissed. "Will you knock it off?"

One of the women produced a flashlight, flicked it on and walked to a small room off the main lobby. From the room came the snap of switches being thrown, and the lobby was bathed in dusky, yellow light.

"That little stairway leads to the projection booth," Anne said, gesturing toward a side doorway, as the group moved through swinging double doors and into the theater's auditorium. The air carried light dust and a hint of mildew, and the dusty film on the overhead bulbs gave the room light a subdued and shadowy look. Still, the theater looked much the same as any other theater. All the seats were still there, as though waiting for an audience. Large velvet curtains, secured with scarlet cords, still hung on each side of the screen. The girls were silent as they moved slowly around the space, touching the curtains, examining the seats.

"Amazing," whispered Patty, as one of the chaperones strung a long extension cord from an outlet in the lobby down to the small projector, which now rested on a table in the aisle.

"I didn't know you liked *Bride of Frankenstein* so well," Anne said, "or I would have brought it. Instead, I've got *Creature from the Black Lagoon.*"

"Great!" laughed Marie. "I love that one, too." She paused as an idea hit her. "Hey, Anne. Do you suppose we could . . . maybe . . . take a peek in the projection room? You know, where that woman . . . ?"

"Marie!" Patty said. "Are you crazy?"

"Well, what the heck," Marie said, smiling. "It was years ago."

Anne shrugged. "It really doesn't matter to me. Not much in there." As she moved toward the small stairs in the lobby, all the girls crowded in behind her. No one spoke as they shuffled and bumped up the narrow staircase, bathed in weak light from a single bulb.

"Well, that's it," Anne said as she pushed open the narrow door and flipped another light switch. "Just a projection booth. Nothing more." Pushing and straining to get a view, the girls saw only a small, very dusty room with a few dust-laden film cans and pieces of equipment lying about. The huge, clunky-looking projector was still in place, aimed at a front wall in which there were two or three large, rectangular openings. A large and exquisitely delicate lacework of cobwebs stretched from the extended arms of the projector to a nearby table. Several of the girls glanced at the ceiling, with its steel beam running side to side, then quickly looked away.

❏ "I love the part where Julie Adams takes a swim in the lagoon, and we know that horrible Gill-Man is down there, but she doesn't," Marie said as the girls filed back into the main auditorium. One of the chaperones began adjusting a reel of *Creature from the Black Lagoon* on the projector on the table in the aisle as the girls dusted off the surrounding theater seats.

"Take some snacks," Anne said, smiling, as she handed out bags of chips and cans of soda. "All we have is the feature movie. No newsreel."

"What the heck's a newsreel?" asked Cathy.

Anne smiled. "In the old days, before a theater showed the main feature, they always showed a short film that had news of the day. It was before people started getting most of their news pictures from television. After everyone had a TV, theaters stopped showing newsreels."

"She loves to tell stuff from the old days that she learned from her grandfather," Marie whispered.

At first, the whirring sound of the little projector was distracting, but soon the girls were unaware of it as the black-and-white images of the film flickered across the surface of the old theater screen. At the first sign of the Gill-Man slipping through the treacherous waters of the dreaded Black Lagoon, several girls gasped. Even the eyes of the chaperones were riveted on the screen now, with the crunch of chips and gulps of soda the only occasional counterpoint to the projector noise and on-screen dialogue.

"No!" Marie cried out, as the monster reached out of the water toward a hapless human. At that moment, the theater lights suddenly went out and the little projector ground to a stop.

Now the pitch-black auditorium echoed with the screams of other girls, punctuated by the voices of the two chaperones urging them to be calm and remain in their seats.

"It's just an electrical failure," said one of the women. "Nothing to be afraid of. I'll take the flashlight back and see if I can get the lights back on. Please! Please stop screaming!"

Before the woman could rise from her seat, a rumble and whir began in the old theater's projection booth, followed by the rising hum of the big projector. A spear of light stabbed from the projection booth, filling the entire theater screen with the bright flash of a vintage newsreel. All the girls and the women jumped as an old-time narrator's voice rattled from the sound system.

"In news of the day," the voice said, "several hundred people attended ribbon-cutting ceremonies marking the opening of the beautiful and elegant new Galaxy Theater, built by real-estate developer Wilfred Strebner, shown here with scissors in hand . . ."

The image on the screen showed a smiling, middle-aged man cutting a broad sash draped across the doors of the theater as other smiling men and women applauded. All were dressed in quaint, older-fashioned clothes.

"Hey! That's this place!" Marie said, her voice wavering.

The voice from the speakers stopped and the news film faded as a different set of images began to move across the huge, old theater screen. Now, instead of the smiling people at the ribbon-cutting ceremony, there were two people, a young man and a young woman, half in shadows, kissing as large film reels turned behind them.

"That's the projection booth," said one of the girls. "And that's the old projector. But who are those people?" Almost as if on cue, the picture zeroed in on the faces of the two people as they stopped kissing and smiled tenderly at each other.

Anne shrieked and put her hand to her mouth. "My father!" she hissed. "He looks so *young* . . ."

"Oh, my," gasped one of the chaperones. "She's the . . ."

"Projectionist," said the other chaperone, her voice wavering.

"Oh, this is awful," cried Anne. "What is going on?" Just as she spoke, the screen image switched to the same young projectionist, alone in the booth, scowling as she worked to adjust the reels on the machine. From behind her, a pair of woman's hands holding a slim rope reached out, looped the rope around her neck and yanked it tight. The girl struggled furiously, her eyes rolling, trying desperately to free herself. Finally, her body went limp.

The killer stepped on a chair, looped the rope around the steel beam in the tiny room and began hoisting the girl's body upward. As the killer turned and strained to lift the burden, her face was visible for the merest fraction of a second. It was a young face, barely more than a teenager, but there was no mistaking it: the face was that of Anne's mother.

Anne, still crying, began beating the back of the seat in front of her. "What *is* this? Some kind of sick joke?" she sobbed.

Once more the image faded, and in its place were two people dancing, smiling, as an orchestra played in the background and other couples danced nearby. Anne's parents, a few years older, moved and swayed as this image faded, replaced by the lights, laughter and smiles of a wedding reception, with Anne's parents dancing again as bride and groom.

A moment or two later, the screen went black and the dusky yellow theater lights came back on.

"I think it's time we got out of here," said a chaperone, her voice still wavering a little, as she walked toward the theater lobby. "I don't know what's happening here, but I'll feel better if we have the party back at Anne's house."

All of the girls remained in their seats, stunned, for a moment or two, then they jumped and ran toward the lobby, after the chaperone.

"I want to know who's behind this," the second chaperone said. She followed the girls, then turned and started up the stairs toward the projection booth, holding her flashlight like a club. All of the girls followed her, jamming into the narrow passageway. When they reached the little room, it seemed at first that nothing had changed. The old projector remained dusty and silent, and the cobwebs still formed a delicate bridge between the projector and the table.

A moment later, one of the girls crowded into the doorway beside the chaperone raised a shaking hand and pointed, her face a speechless mask of horror. At the far side of the projector, barely visible and faintly luminous in the dim light, was the figure of the young projectionist from the newsreel, staring at them, one delicate hand resting on the ancient machine. She nodded slowly without changing expression, then slowly began to fade until she had disappeared.

For a moment, all was silent. Then, in unison, the girls began to scream again, tumbling and jostling pell-mell down the narrow staircase toward the lobby.

❏ The shrieking explosion of noise still echoed in Patty's ears as she opened her eyes. Foggy from sleep, she sat up halfway, and was greeted by a scene of devastation: candy wrappers, crumpled bags from chips, empty soda cans, and girls draped over, beside, and on the leather furniture in Anne's family's immense family room.

Now Patty's friend, Cathy, was awake, too. She squinted at Patty through one sleep-heavy eye. "We must have gone to sleep about four this morning," she rasped. "What time is it?"

"Almost noon."

"After the monster movies and all the junk food, it's a wonder anyone got to sleep at all."

Marie and several of the other girls were awake now, too. "Boy, am I tired!" Marie croaked, shifting her weight on the leather sofa. "Maybe it's a good thing we didn't vote to go to the theater. My back would have felt even worse in those seats."

"Speaking of the theater," Cathy said, "I had the most horrible dream."

"Me, too," said Patty.

"I did, too," Marie chimed in.

"I think I beat you all," Anne said, yawning. "I had the most awful, most terrible, most ridiculous dream I've ever had. I dreamed we *did* go to the old theater."

"That's funny. So did I," Patty said.

"Me, too," said the other girls.

"My dream was terrible," said Cathy. "We were watching a movie, and then the lights went out, and some kind of news thing came on and it was scary. It showed that girl—you know, that projectionist we talked about before, and . . ."

Now everyone was looking at Anne, whose eyes were beginning to brim over with tears. "We all had the *same dream*?" she whispered. "The *same one*?"

"This is strange, just too strange," Marie whispered, dabbing at her own eyes. "It's like the dead girl was maybe trying to . . ."

"*Mother!*" Anne gasped, running to the door leading to the hall. "Mother! Please! Will you come in here? *Mother . . . !*"

THE SHOOTING

"If this were 1870 or 1880, you'd be riding along in a hot, rattling stagecoach, surrounded by the smells of dust and horses," Paul's dad said from the front seat. He gripped the steering wheel of the family van with one hand while he reached back with a tourist brochure for Paul and his sister, Laura.

"Although the life was hard," Paul read aloud from the brochure, "people all over the world are interested in the American frontier of a century past, with its gunfighters and cowboys and robbers and pioneers."

Paul and Laura's dad loved to talk about what he called the "Old West." For the past couple of days, since they'd left Yellowstone Park, he had talked of the Gene Autry Western Heritage Museum in Los Angeles, near the city's zoo and Griffith Park.

"I can't wait to see this place," his dad had said. "You can see the *actual* guns and saddles used by people like Billy the Kid and Buffalo Bill Cody and Wyatt Earp. Imagine! It's like a trip back in time!"

Paul's mother smiled. "I don't think your dad ever grew out of his 'cowboy' phase," she said, patting him on the arm.

In truth, Paul had never been very interested in western history or in museums. But this museum sounded special. He was surprised how large and beautiful the museum looked when they arrived. From the broad plaza in front, he could see lines of schoolchildren boarding buses across the street in the Los Angeles Zoo's huge asphalt parking lot.

"That's Gene Autry," their dad said, pointing at a large bronze statue as they entered the museum's inner courtyard. "He was called a 'singing cowboy,' and starred in many movies long before you were born. Later he became very successful in business. Because he loved the American West, he wanted to build a great Western History museum. And that's just what he did."

The inside of the museum was immense, with beautiful, vaulted ceilings, polished floors, and large rooms on two levels filled with items from the past. Already, Paul had decided that maybe museums weren't so bad after all; in fact, this was probably the most interesting museum he'd ever seen.

In one display, he learned that people set foot in the western United States as early as 13,000 years ago. Other displays contained buckskin clothing, Native American headdresses, and even a stuffed, full-sized bison bull and a longhorn steer.

On the lower level, Paul couldn't believe his eyes. Each new room, each area, held items he had never seen before. He saw personal items once owned by Capt. Myles Keogh and Lt. Col. George Armstrong Custer, who died fighting Indians at the great Battle of the Little Bighorn in Montana. Nearby was an original, full-size stagecoach pulled by four stuffed horses. In another room was an actual, full-size chuck wagon with cooks rustling up food for hungry cowboys. Still other rooms held saddles, boots, chaps, and more guns—some of them priceless weapons with inlaid gold, originally given to presidents and kings.

"You *still* haven't seen it all," whispered Paul's dad as he tugged on his son's sleeve. "Remember me telling you about the famous Old West lawman, Wyatt Earp, and his gambler friend, Doc Holliday? Well, right here, they've got the actual guns carried by those men so many years ago." Paul noticed that his dad was as excited as he was. "And there's a display showing the famous Gunfight at the O.K. Corral."

Paul remembered his dad talking many times in the past about this most famous of all Old West gunfights. Dozens of books had been written, he said, and movies had been made about the fight on the dusty streets of Tombstone, Arizona, on a warm October day in 1881. He had told Paul how the Earp brothers—Wyatt, Virgil, and Morgan—and their friend, Doc Holliday, had shot it out with several cowboys with whom they'd had a disagreement. When it was over, three of the cowboys—Tom and Frank McLaury and Billy Clanton—lay dead, and Virgil and Morgan Earp were badly wounded.

As Paul thought about this, and what that terrible day must have been like, Laura ran up, pulling their mother by the hand. "They've got something called the Los Angeles *Times* Children's Discovery Gallery over there," she puffed, "where they let kids try on clothes and you can touch stuff! That's where *I'm* going to be."

"Come on," Paul's dad said, motioning and pointing. He and Paul entered a large room, one entire end of which was covered by an authentic, antique Old West saloon bar, complete with brass railing, spittoons, a large mirror, and figures of large, demure ladies hand-carved into the frame. Paul could almost hear the sounds of a dozen men's voices, and maybe a woman or two, all talking and laughing over the rolling rhythm of a tinkling piano. It was easy to imagine the pungent musk of cigar smoke, mixed with sweat, horse smells, whiskey, and leather.

At the other end of the room were several "gaming" tables at which cowboys once gambled in games of keno, faro, poker, and roulette.

Past the tables and beyond a railing were nine

full-size figures, grim-looking men holding guns and dressed in the dark coats and dark, flat hats of another century. These represented the Earp brothers, Doc Holliday, and the cowboys, all riveted in place in a silent dance of death for all eternity.

As Paul walked up, his dad was peering intently into a glass case on a far wall. He motioned for Paul to come closer. Inside the case, no more than a foot from Paul's nose, was a short, double-barreled shotgun once carried by Wyatt Earp. Above the shotgun was the Colt revolver carried by Doc Holliday. Near it was a Smith & Wesson revolver with fancy scrollwork engraved into the frame, barrel, and cylinder. "Wyatt Earp may have carried this gun at the O.K. Corral," a sign said. Below the guns was a page of notebook paper with a diagram of the gunfight, drawn in pencil by Earp many years after the fight.

"Can you believe this?" Paul's dad whispered. "We're only inches away from guns that wrote history on the streets of old Tombstone."

Just then another museum visitor punched a button on the railing and a recorded voice began a narrative of the fight. Paul and his dad listened for a few minutes until the speaker was silent, and then his dad said, "Be right back. I'd better go pay some attention to Laura."

As the other museum visitors moved on, Paul stood alone, leaning on the rail and watching the silent, grim-looking figures. There was something strange and fascinating about the way they remained frozen in time, guns in hand, poised on the edge of disaster. It seemed all the more strange now, as the other visitors moved away and their subdued murmurs drifted into a momentary silence.

Paul sneezed. "Excuse me," he muttered to no one, then sneezed again. Must be dust in the air, he thought, although he hadn't noticed it before in the modern, spotless museum. His throat felt a little scratchy from whatever was in the air, and he was becoming very warm now, too. Where before the museum's light had been subdued, now he was blinded by light, so bright it blocked out the guns, the walls, everything. He blinked his eyes, which were beginning to water from the bright light.

Echoing sounds now had begun around and over him, a growing jumble of voices, the rattle and creak of wagons, and—was is possible?—the clap! clup! hoof sounds and occasional whinny of horses. Even his clothes were different. Where before he'd had on jeans, a T-shirt, and hightops, now he had on a wrinkled, off-white, long-sleeved shirt, scratchy dark pants with suspenders, and strange-looking ankle-high leather shoes.

As he strained to adjust his sight in the blinding light, two men walked past, but their steps were not the near-silent whisper of shoes on carpeted museum floors. They scuffed past, heavy boots on uneven ground. Both were dressed alike: baggy, dark-woolen

61

pants stuffed into heavy boots, broad suspenders, rough-cut shirts, and flat, broad-brimmed dark hats. Both had a several-days' growth of beard on craggy, sun-hardened faces.

"It don't seem good," one man was saying. "Them cowboys is scared and mad, and you know the other side ain't gonna back down. Somebody's gonna get shot."

Fighting a growing sense of panic, his eyes still watering from the blinding sun and the acrid street dust in the air, Paul stumbled after the two men. "Excuse me," he blurted out, "could you tell me where I am?"

The men continued on without hearing. Turning, he noticed that he was standing almost squarely in front of a plain, unadorned barber shop, identified by a large wooden sign protruding outward, toward the street. A newspaper lying on a wooden chair just outside the door bore the name *Tombstone Epitaph* in fancy, old-fashioned lettering. Below that was printed "Tombstone, Arizona Territory." Looking more closely at the paper, Paul's heart almost stopped. It was dated Wednesday, October 26, 1881.

"Looks like trouble, for sure," he heard someone say. Peering inside, Paul saw that the speaker was a barber, who had stopped shaving a man momentarily to stare out of the shop toward a gathering crowd a block or so away.

The barber was staring not only at the crowd, but

also at four somber men not far from Paul, between the shop and the more distant crowd. Slowly, he walked beyond the men and stared at the people down the block.

Looking back, toward the four men, Paul felt a chill of anticipation. Something terrible, something momentous, was at hand. The four somber men all wore long, dark coats; now Paul noticed that three had guns visible under their coats, and one of those was carrying a shotgun at his side. The fourth had his hand in his coat pocket, as though holding a gun out of sight. Each wore a black string tie, white shirt, and a flat, black Stetson hat. As he watched, the four began to move in slow, silent procession, past him toward the gathering down the street.

"You might want to be careful," Paul suddenly blurted out. "I heard someone say somebody was going to get shot." He didn't know why he'd said it. Something about the men, maybe, and their somber bearing.

The man with his hand in his pocket, a tall, slim man with a handlebar mustache, turned to Paul for only a fraction of a moment. He said nothing, then nodded, and the quickest, faintest flicker of a smile crossed his lips before he returned to the business at hand and moved with his companions toward the street corner.

Paul was riveted, and his heart was racing. He followed the men, keeping pace with them, making certain he stayed well behind. Their pace was deliberate, almost leisurely.

As they reached the corner of the next dirt street and glanced to the left, several people nearby scattered for shelter behind a surrounding cluster of rough-hewn buildings. Peering down the same street, from behind the men, Paul saw three or four cowboys, one clutching the reins of a horse. They were angry and agitated, their gaze fixed on the four somber men now approaching them.

Paul walked a few paces more behind the men, then stopped. In a corner of his vision, he was aware of several bystanders, well off to the side, scattering and hiding behind nearby buildings. He stood transfixed, unable to move, watching the men in long coats move closer to the cowboys.

As the men approached, the cowboys shifted a few paces toward an open lot between two buildings. Behind and off to the side of the buildings was a large, fenced enclosure containing several horses. The fence reached all the way to the street, where there was a broad gate. A sign on a nearby post read O.K. Corral. From the street, Paul could still see a couple of the cowboys, and the one cowboy's horse, which was clearly agitated and nervous.

As the four men reached the cowboys and turned toward the open lot, Paul heard someone curse. Almost instantly the air was filled with the deafening, reverberating roar of several guns firing, almost at once. A cloud of drifting smoke now covered the street as the roar came again and again, all in the space of a few seconds. Paul saw one of the men stagger and fall while another fell to one knee, still firing. Another staggered into the street from the lot and fell, then raised slightly and fired again, almost directly in Paul's direction.

The horse that before had been so nervous now bolted and ran, straight toward him as still more shots were fired. Gasping in the sudden shock and confusion, his eyes riveted on the horse, Paul dived toward the side of the street, slamming into a hitching post as the frantic animal thundered past. He dropped to one knee, then sank to the rutted ground. Struggling again to rise, he felt a wrenching pain in his shoulder as the black of unconsciousness settled over him like a satin shroud.

❑ "Signs are good. Everything is stable." It was a man's voice, distant, tiny, as though heard through a long, narrow tube. "This is Dr. Johnston, Paul. Can you hear me?"

Slowly, very deliberately, he opened his eyes. He was in a stark, white bed, with what seemed like a tight sheet covering most of his body. He was enveloped instantly by his mother's and father's arms as his mother kissed him on the forehead.

"Welcome back," Paul's dad said, as Paul opened his eyes, then closed them again in the harsh light of the room. He tried to shift his weight, but was unable to move. Attempting to roll to his side, he realized that his entire left shoulder and arm were immobile, held in place by bandages that covered much of his upper body.

When he opened his mouth to speak, the sound was little more than a rasp. A nurse gave him a small piece of ice to moisten his mouth, and motioned that he shouldn't try and speak just yet.

"You've been in surgery, and then asleep, for most of two days," his dad said.

"What . . . why . . . what happened?" Paul managed to whisper.

"Well . . ." Paul's dad looked at his mother. "You were shot, son. It all happened so fast. Just after you and I looked at the saloon bar and the old guns, we found Laura and your mother and left the museum. We were going to wind up a great day by going to a nice restaurant for dinner. We barely got to the parking lot when a car went past. People in it were shooting guns. I suppose they were after rival gang members. The police said they were probably using automatic weapons."

"And I got hit?" Paul whispered.

"You got hit," his dad said. "You even got in the newspaper."

"I'm so sick of gangs," sighed Paul's mother. "Terrible thing when a family can't even go to a museum in a perfectly good part of town without risking a drive-by shooting."

Paul's dad held up a newspaper for Paul to see. "I can read the whole story to you later," he said, smiling a little.

"That's pretty incredible," Paul said. His voice sounded low and scratchy. "I don't remember . . ."

"They tell us," his mother said gently, "that it's pretty common in things like this for the person to completely block everything out, you know, in your memory, everything that happened just before . . ."

"It could have been a lot worse for you, and for all of us. You could have been killed if it hadn't been for the strange-looking guy in the park," his dad said, glancing at Paul's mother. "That's in the newspaper story, too."

"Stranger?" Paul whispered.

"A man stepped from the trees in Griffith Park and opened fire with a handgun. Several shots hit the car. Took the gang members by surprise. Their shots went wild except the one that winged your shoulder. The man disappeared as the car raced away. According to a couple of witnesses, he was tall, had a long, handlebar mustache, and had on a long, dark coat and a dark, western-style hat. Police searched the park, but they couldn't find him."

"We're just glad you're alive," Paul's mother said.

❏ "I want to go back to the museum," Paul said a week later, as his parents helped him into the van to begin the trip home.

"Paul, really," his mother began, her expression suddenly very serious. "I mean, of all the places . . . I think we should start back for home, and put this all behind us."

"Mom and Dad, *please*." He wasn't even sure why he wanted this. Maybe it was the way things had all tumbled together. Maybe he just wanted to see that the museum was really a peaceful place, and the shooting had just been a freak accident. But he knew he wanted to go back, more than anything, if only for a few minutes.

"I guess there's one thing," his dad said after a long pause. "If he doesn't go back, maybe it'll remain this terrible thing in his memory. If he does go, maybe we can all close the book on it."

The museum was as beautiful, and as peaceful, as before. Family members strolled quietly among the displays, murmuring to each other and pointing at interesting discoveries.

As Paul reached the O.K. Corral display, with his parents and Laura following, his heart was racing a little and he felt a few beads of perspiration forming on his forehead. Slowly, tentatively, he approached the railing as another museum visitor pushed the button, and again he listened to the narrative describing the famous gunfight. Everything seemed just as before, completely normal. He began to relax a little, and even thought himself a little silly for getting tense the way he had.

Turning away from the figures, he approached the gun display in the glass case below the enlarged photo of Wyatt Earp. This time Paul felt a brief, fleeting spark of familiarity, of recognition that sent an odd chill down his spine. How could he tell his parents that this was the same face that had nodded slightly at him, and almost smiled? He bent down, just as he had before, with his nose no more than a few inches from the famous weapons. Leaning a little closer, he peered intently at one of the revolvers resting on the transparent supports. It was no longer balanced, but instead slightly askew, as though recently handled. A smeared hand print was visible on the polished steel of the gun's frame, and slight, gray-white traces—powder marks, from firing—were just barely visible on the front of the cylinder.

NANTUCKET
SLEIGH RIDE

■ Picking up, once again, her teacher's battered copy of *Moby Dick* by Herman Melville, Sheila could still hear the words of Mr. Foster, who had taught her eighth-grade English class during the past year: "Over the summer, if you want to read something that's *really* challenging, try this. It's a long, difficult, nineteenth-century book about whales and whaling, and it's never, or rarely, offered to students younger than high school or college. Some parts of it you'll find boring, and you won't understand parts of it. But you are very bright, and much of the book is wonderful. If you finish, you'll be able to say you've read one of the finest, and greatest, novels ever written."

Sitting beside her parents' pool in San Diego, with the late-afternoon California sun just beginning to dip toward the sea out beyond Point Loma, she wasn't certain she'd ever finish this huge volume, at least not before school began again in the fall. It was especially difficult with the swim meet coming up in a few weeks. She was training daily, often for hours, sometimes in the pool at home, more often in the larger pool at the athletic club. The training usually left her with too little time—or simply too tired—to do much reading.

She really wanted to be able to stop by the middle school—her old school—in the fall and tell Mr. Foster she'd finished the book. So far, however, the scrap of paper she used as a bookmark was stuck less than fifty pages into the story, near a funny scene in which the narrator, Ishmael, meets Queequeg, the savage harpooneer.

She wished she'd had more time to read the book. On the other hand, a first- or second-place finish in this meet's freestyle competition would guarantee her a spot on her new school's swim team, and make her swim club members very happy.

If this wasn't all, her Uncle Charlie—her favorite uncle—would be here for dinner in less than two hours. Every time he came into town, he stopped by for dinner. And when he did, Sheila wanted time to be with him. Charlie was a little older than Sheila's dad. He was divorced, with no children, so he liked to visit and send cards and letters to Sheila's family as though it were his own. He was interesting and fun to talk to, and had seen many of the world's port cities and countries as a professional merchant sailor.

Every time he visited, he brought with him new tales of strange and exotic people and places. She couldn't wait to tell him about *Moby Dick*, since Charlie had worked on a few whaling boats early in his career.

"I'll be on the *Jon Regis*, a 20,000-ton cargo vessel, this time, bound for Australia," Charlie said later that evening over dinner, when Sheila asked him the name of his ship. "She's been in dry dock here in San Diego to get a few repairs on her hull. We'll be taking her to Honolulu first, then down past Fiji and around through the Tasman Sea to Melbourne on the south coast."

It sounded so interesting. Sheila wished desperately that she could go on one of these voyages, and see the kinds of people and ports that Charlie saw. Charlie, on the other hand, loved to tell his favorite niece about strange and interesting places. His sun-leathered face would crinkle in a smile as he spun the stories and made this point or that point. At the end of his stories, he always winked at Sheila. Her mother and father loved to hear Charlie's stories, too.

"I'm reading *Moby Dick*," she said now, during a pause in the conversation. "Maybe I'll learn something about whales and the old-time whaling ships."

"Fantastic!" Charlie said, nodding. "Although old-time whaling was mighty different from the kind I did. But *whales*—now *there*'s some creatures that haven't changed for thousands of years. They're mammals, and they breathe air. A lot of experts figure they originally were land animals, millions of years ago, before they adapted to the sea. Truly interesting animals, that's for certain."

"They sure are big," Sheila said, smiling.

"Big?" Charlie laughed. "You can't even imagine how big. Did you know the biggest animal that ever lived is living today? And it's even bigger than any dinosaur that ever lived. That animal's a female blue whale. She can be over 100 feet long and weigh 200 *tons*. That's more than a hundred automobiles, stacked one on top of the other, or more than *thirty large elephants*! And yet," Charlie moved his hand in a slow, smooth arc over his dinner plate, "she can move through water as smooth as an eagle riding a wind current in the high Rockies."

Sheila found it hard to imagine any living creature that heavy. "*Moby Dick* is really hard to read," she said, "but I *did* think it was awfully funny when Queequeg, the harpooneer and cannibal, scares the heck out of poor Ishmael."

"Yeah, 150 years ago old-time whaling was big business," Charlie said. "A good harpooneer, who was basically a good spear-thrower, was an extremely valuable crew member, and he got paid better than an ordinary sailor. In this century, nobody had to throw a harpoon. For a long time now, they've had harpoon cannons, big guns, to do the job." Charlie finished his coffee and pushed his chair back a little. "I'll tell you something interesting. You ever hear of the term, 'Nantucket sleigh ride'?"

Sheila shook her head, and so did her parents.

She'd heard of people riding sleighs in the snow, and Santa's sleigh, but not whatever Charlie was talking about.

"Back in the old days, whaling ships went out on years-long voyages to hunt whales for their oil. That whale oil was worth lots of money. It was used mostly to light lamps before there was electricity or kerosene. The sperm whale was the best source. It had the finest oil, and the most. It's a giant animal, and its huge head has a big cavity full of oil, besides the thousands of pounds of blubber under the skin. After they killed the whale, the old-time sailors melted down the blubber, and took hundreds of gallons of oil from the sperm whale's head. Other types of whales were taken, too, by the tens of thousands, until this century, when countries started limiting the number that could be taken. And, of course, there isn't the same demand now."

"Do they still hunt them?" Sheila asked.

"Well, most countries have outlawed hunting, but some are still being taken."

"It seems like they should stop, now that there aren't as many whales left," Sheila said.

"Well, to get back to my story," Charlie said, "sperm whales like old Moby Dick are huge, and sometimes dangerous, animals—more than 50 feet long and weighing more than 50 tons. Sailors used to tell stories about them, and some sailors wondered if these great beasts ever tried to even the score with man."

"I guess I can't blame them," Sheila said.

Charlie shrugged. "In the old sailing days, when a ship would spot one moving slowly, sort of relaxing on the sea surface, they'd lower a slim, little boat, called a 'Yankee whaleboat,' into the water with six brave sailors in it. They'd row the little boat as close as possible to the whale, and a harpooneer in the bow would drive the razor-sharp point of the harpoon deep into the animal."

"That's *terrible*!" gasped Sheila.

"Well," said Charlie, "they *were* out there to kill whales. Anyway, the iron head of the harpoon was attached to long coils of slim Manila rope, which was snugged around a thick post, called a loggerhead, in the stern—the rear part—of the boat. The frightened, angry whale usually took off at high speed, often going into a deep dive called 'sounding.' When it did, it pulled the little boat through the waves at high speed, with the sailors hanging on for their lives. The loggerhead kept tension on the line, and sooner or later the whale wore himself out and came to the surface. That's when another sailor, skilled with a long, spearlike weapon called a lance, would drive the lance deep into the animal and kill it."

The thought of all this was making Sheila a little sick. "But why," she said, almost in a whisper, "did the sailors call it a . . . ?"

"Nantucket sleigh ride?" Charlie said, patting her on the hand. "The little island of Nantucket, off the coast of Massachusetts, was a premier whaling port 150 years ago. For a while it was the port where most American whalers set off on their voyages. That's why the sailors jokingly called this hair-raising, death-defying experience a 'Nantucket sleigh ride.' "

"I'd never heard that," said Sheila's mother, as she poured Charlie another cup of coffee. "It had to be terribly dangerous."

"It was," Charlie laughed. "Whales like that have been known to smash little boats, and even ram their huge heads into the old-time wooden ships. And when the rope was spinning out of the little boat at extremely high speed, it was capable of cutting off a man's hand or dragging him out to sea if he got caught in it. The sailors usually wore pads on the palms of their hands to shield against terrible burns as they handled the high-speed line."

As Charlie and her parents chatted about other things, Sheila wandered out to the backyard and sat down by the pool. Underwater lights gave the pool a glassy, peaceful look. She felt at home here. In another way, she felt at home in the water whenever she swam, too, even as she was puffing and straining to build her strength and endurance. The whales certainly had to feel at home in the water. How terrible it was that men had come so often to the whales' home to kill and rip them apart. She was glad Charlie had become a different kind of sailor.

Her uncle still had a couple of days in town before

he shipped out, so Sheila knew he'd be back for dinner again at least one more time. She decided this time she'd try and get him to talk about the strange, faraway places he'd been, and not talk about whales.

The next day, practicing in the club pool, she kept imagining a mammoth whale, lolling in the vast waters of some ocean, unaware that humans were about to drive a harpoon deep into its body. It was a terrible thought. And the more she thought about it, the angrier she became.

That evening, when Charlie showed up for dinner again, she tried not to let her anger show. She wanted Charlie to have a nice dinner before he left. Still, it was hard to forget about the whales. "You ever go through the Panama Canal?" she asked, as Charlie sliced through a steak just off the charcoal grill.

"You bet!" Charlie said, smiling as always. "Want to know something interesting about that canal?"

"Sure." She smiled. Charlie loved to tell her strange, interesting facts.

"Well, you know that the canal links the Caribbean Sea and Atlantic Ocean on the east side with the Pacific Ocean on the west side. Saves ships the trouble of going all the way around Cape Horn, at the bottom of South America, to get from one to the other."

"Yes." Sheila had known this since fifth- or sixth-grade geography.

"Well, did you know that the Pacific end of the

canal is actually farther *east* than the Atlantic end?"

"Wait a minute." Sheila scowled. "That doesn't make sense."

Charlie laughed. "Yes, it does, because the canal runs mostly north-to-south, not east-to-west." He swung a piece of steak on his fork through the air to make his point. "Anyway, I thought you'd find that interesting."

After dinner, she again went out by the pool while her parents and Charlie talked. She felt a little sad, both because she wouldn't see Charlie again for a while, and because she couldn't forget the whales.

❑ "Such a long face." Charlie's voice startled her. Nearly an hour had gone by since she'd finished dinner. She turned in the lounge chair to see Charlie's face, smiling as usual.

"I feel bad about something," she blurted out suddenly, not wanting to hold it in any longer. "I know it's silly, but I still feel terrible about the whales."

Charlie surprised her by throwing his head back and laughing. "*That's* all that's bothering you?" he said, still laughing a little. He put a gentle hand on her shoulder. "Listen," he said quietly, his face more serious. "Whales are a product, something to be harvested and sold, just like cattle or wheat or eggs. When I first went to sea, I was just a kid, and I sure helped kill more than my share. But it was a living, nothing more. People talk about dwindling herds, but

I don't buy that 'endangered species' baloney. There are more than eighty different kinds o' whales, and believe me, there are plenty still in the sea."

Sheila must have looked a little shocked. "I hope you don't hate me because I was a whaler," he said softly. His tone was more serious now. "Some sailors have called whales a dark force of nature," he said. "I don't know. But I do know those old boys can carry a grudge, and I do know they can kill you. Look what happened to Captain Ahab's ship, the *Pequod*, in *Moby Dick*. The whale sent it straight to Davy Jones' locker."

"But that's only a story . . ." she began.

Charlie interrupted her. "Old sailors will tell you it's happened in real life, too, where one of these beasts has tried to sink a ship and kill the crew. The truth is, I could shoot a harpoon straight into a whale right now, today, and it wouldn't bother me a bit." He tapped the back of Sheila's chair for emphasis. "We own the sea," he said. "They don't."

❏ Days later, after Charlie had shipped out once again, Sheila and her friend, Denise, were relaxing in the warm sun with Denise's parents on Silver Strand Beach in Coronado, across the bay from San Diego. "It always amazes me when I sit here and look out to sea," Denise said, shielding her eyes, "that there's basically nothing but water between here and Japan. Just thousands of miles of ocean."

Sheila closed her eyes and leaned back, listening

to the rhythm of the rolling surf, punctuated by the cries of sea birds. "My main worry right now isn't thousands of miles of ocean," she murmured. "It's a hundred meters of pool water."

Denise and her parents laughed. "I think you'll be relieved when that swim meet is over, won't you?" Denise's mom said.

Sheila nodded. The meet had been hanging over her head for so long, it *would* be a relief when it was done, regardless of what happened. She couldn't even relax on the beach without worrying about it. She sighed, tossed her sunglasses on a nearby towel and sprinted toward the gently rolling waves.

Ocean swimming was a lot different from swimming in a pool. For one thing, occasional riptides—currents that could carry a swimmer out to sea—made it more dangerous. On the other hand, ocean swimming was a good muscle- and endurance-builder. Besides, she'd learned long ago that a swimmer could escape a riptide simply by swimming parallel to the shore. Most people got in trouble by trying to swim *toward* the shore, which didn't work with these capricious currents.

It was a struggle getting beyond the rolling surf, but once she reached deeper water the ocean felt more peaceful. The blue-green surface moved with a broad, living rhythm that hadn't changed in a hundred million years. She rolled to her back, coasting and resting, then flipped back again and resumed a smooth, overhand stroke. The sun, which had blinded her on the beach with its knifelike intensity, now felt merely warm, even comforting. She was well away from shore, but she felt strong and fresh.

She was about to roll slowly onto her back again, enjoying herself, when she realized that she, and the water around her, were now blanketed by a shadow that she assumed was caused by a cloud floating between her and the sun.

Feeling the force of a new, insistent current, she turned again in the water, and nearly fainted with shock as she confronted the cause of the shadow. Yawning before her, barnacles and seaweed still clinging to its slick, rubbery skin, was a great whale. Inside the cavernous mouth, large enough to swallow Sheila whole, were rows of pointed, peglike teeth, each more than six inches long.

In the brief, horrible moment that this giant creature, its mouth still open wide, paused before her in the water, she saw the iron shaft and part of the wooden handle of an old, nineteenth-century harpoon protruding from its side, just behind the enormous, 20-foot head. Still attached to the harpoon was a long, frayed, length of narrow Manila rope. It skipped about on the surface of the water as the animal moved.

She opened her mouth to yell, to cry for help, but nothing came out. She was treading water furiously now, trying to determine whether or not she could swim fast enough to escape. To her horror, as she hesitated, still kicking wildly, the frayed rope whipped through the air in a sizzling arc and wrapped itself around her hands and wrists. At the same moment, the whale closed its gaping mouth and with a thunderous splash, slipped below the waves.

Sheila was now in a total panic, tumbling over and over, deeper and deeper into the cold depths of the ocean, yanked along by the rope. With her lungs nearly bursting, she fought desperately to unwrap the rope from her wrists, already feeling herself sliding into unconsciousness. She almost managed to untie the rope before it yanked her again, farther down, deeper into the silent abyss. As her eyes began to cloud over, the enormous force of the whale pulled her erratically from side to side, upward, then deeper and back again. Streaking past her, in a blur of vision, she saw manta rays, groupers, puffer fish, and squid.

As her vision began to go black, the animal suddenly turned and, using its great head, pushed her gently toward the ocean surface. Coughing, struggling, and crying, Sheila gulped air as the rope released its grip on her wrists. The mammoth animal shifted, moving slowly beside her until one tiny eye was only inches from her face. Its head was now a dark-gray wall, blocking everything else in sight.

The whale met her eyes with a deep-set gaze that seemed to reach back to the very beginning of time. For one brief, riveting moment, Sheila felt, and could understand, the depth of feelings coming from this great creature. "Why?" it seemed to be saying. "Why have they killed us, when there is no need? We are not a dark force in the world, and we are not the enemy." In moments, the whale sank from sight, leaving only a wide, gently spinning whirlpool that quickly faded into the ocean's undulating surface.

❏ "Sheila!" The voice was gentle but insistent, coming from a far corner of her consciousness. "Sheila! Time to head home. Wake up. Sheila!"

She opened her eyes, still stunned with thoughts of the whale. Her neck was sore from leaning back on the sand chair, and the sun was hot on her skin.

"You were tired, dear," Denise's mom said, smiling. "You fell asleep without even getting your toes wet, and now it's time to go home."

She stumbled to her feet, twisted her neck a little to try and get the kinks out, then gathered her things and began to walk with Denise and her parents back to their car. She still couldn't quite understand what had happened, but she wasn't about to talk about it with Denise's family. At least not yet.

"Thanks," she mumbled, climbing from Denise's parents' car in her own driveway. "I'll call you tomorrow," she added, offering Denise a half-wave.

"Better get some more rest," Denise's mom

smiled as the car backed away. "I think the practice sessions are wearing you out."

☐ Her mother was waiting at the patio door, a handkerchief in one hand, when Sheila came around from the driveway. Her dad was there, too. This seemed odd, especially in the middle of the day. When she came closer, she saw that they both looked very sad, and now she could see the shine of tears on her mother's cheeks.

"Some very bad news," her dad said, his voice barely above a whisper. "They just got word to us an hour or so ago. There's been a terrible accident at sea. It's Uncle Charlie. He's . . . dead."

Sheila gasped, dropping her towel and chair.

"Curious accident, early this morning," her dad said, clearing his throat. "Charlie's ship was only a little over a day out of Honolulu, heading for Melbourne. Not long after sunup, a crewman spotted several whales off the port bow. Charlie wasn't on duty at the time. He ran to get his camera. Maybe he was planning to send the pictures to you. We'll never know. He came back on deck, ran up to the bow and began snapping pictures. Somehow, he leaned too far, or slipped or something. Nobody really knows. He went overboard . . ."

"Oh, no!" Sheila sobbed. "That's terrible!"

"They did everything they could to rescue him, but he slipped below the waves almost immediately.

They don't know why he went down so fast. One of the crew thought he spotted him several hundred yards off the bow shortly after the accident, but he had to be mistaken. That just doesn't make sense."

"This is horrible!" said Sheila, still crying.

Her dad's voice broke for a moment, and he stared off, into the distance. "There's more of this that doesn't make any sense," he said slowly, shaking his head. "The officer I talked to said they didn't find Charlie's body until nearly an hour later, and when they did, he was more than three *miles* from the ship. There were deep rope burns on his hands. It's almost like something got him, and whatever it was, it had a lot of power, and took him for a heck of a ride . . ."

THE HEIST

The pictures seemed to jump out at the boy as he turned the pages of the library volume; heavy, well-groomed men with blinding diamond pinkie rings, wearing suits that seemed to be woven from gossamer strands of the finest silk. Their shoes were gloss-black mirrors. The cars in which the men rode were immaculate, luxurious—and *long*. Each had smoked-glass windows, and looked as though it could hold half of the boy's eighth-grade class at the same time.

He was riveted by these slick, steely eyed men and the flashy, expensively dressed young women who were always clinging to their arms.

Gangsters.

They symbolized a world of power, crime, and money.

He wondered what it was it like to be Bugsy Siegel or Al Capone and walk into an expensive restaurant, with everyone nervous and stepping aside, and other people hurrying to give you the best tables and the best service.

Some of the other photographs in the book on crime showed bloody scenes of gangland war and crumpled, bullet-ridden forms. Still others showed gangsters turning from the camera as they were being led away, in handcuffs, by the police. These scenes seemed jarringly different from the slick suits and big cars and fancy ladies.

"Danny!" His mother's whisper was sharp, yet subdued because of the library. "I've been all over looking for you. What on earth are you doing?"

"Just reading while I waited for you. Just looking at old pictures and stuff."

"Put it back on the shelf. We're late for dinner."

All that evening he thought about the men in the photographs. He wondered how, and why, people got to be gangsters. In spite of the power and money, how terrible it must be, thought Danny, to know that any day you could wind up in jail, or lying in a pool of blood on a sidewalk.

The next day at school, he thought about what it must be like to be rich and powerful, to have enough money to buy anything or go anywhere you wanted. *He* had all he could do to save enough money from his paper route to buy a new catcher's mitt.

He told his friend, Gavin, about the pictures in the library, with the fancy cars and diamond pinkie rings.

His friend shrugged. "Gangsters are in a high-risk

business," he said. "They may get rich, but they may get killed, too."

"No kidding," said Danny's best friend, Tyler, joining in the conversation. "Anybody who thinks crime pays is crazy. Gavin's right. A lot of gangsters and robbers don't live very long."

❏ A few days later, as Danny sat in the shade munching chips and dreaming about yachts and fancy cars, two boys around his age approached him. They were close to his size and had longish hair in the back, just like his. They were dressed better than he was, however. Their jackets alone must have cost two hundred dollars apiece. Their faces weren't familiar. He shifted a little in the grass and waited for them to speak. They watched him for a moment, and in their eyes he saw something that wasn't in the eyes of his friends; it was a cold-eyed intensity, an edge, a hardness. He wondered who they were, what they had done, to give them this look.

"Danny," one of the boys said, finally. He didn't say it as a question, or a greeting. He just said it. There was neither friendliness nor unfriendliness in the tone.

"You guys transfers?" Danny said, shifting his weight again in the grass and putting down his bag of chips. "I haven't seen you around."

"Yeah, we're transfers," the other boy said. "We're new. I'm Wayne. My brother's name is Mike."

Danny nodded, waiting. It still didn't seem as though they'd looked him up just to tell him their names.

Finally the first boy spoke again. "We wondered if you might be interested in seeing some . . . uh . . . action . . ." His tone became lower, softer. "A heist. You know what I mean." He looked around, to make certain no one else was listening.

"A real heist," whispered his brother.

Danny stood up, and he, too, looked around before speaking. "Is this a joke?"

"No joke," said Mike, who seemed to be the older of the two brothers.

Danny smiled, more out of nervousness than anything else. He wasn't sure what to say. Sure, a heist was wrong. Theft could get you in trouble, *big* trouble, with the police. On the other hand, he had always wondered what it was like to be in on a real "job." Maybe it would be sort of like in the movies. It certainly sounded exciting. Besides, maybe he could get enough to buy his mom a real nice present for her next birthday, instead of the little stuff he usually gave her.

He was still smiling. "Yeah," he whispered. "Yeah, I'm interested. But why me?"

"Not that many people around here gutsy enough to take the risk," said Wayne. "We heard you talking about gangsters, and figured you might be curious. And by the way, I wouldn't do any more talking. The fewer people know about this, the better."

He studied them, especially their faces. "You done anything like that before, or are you all talk?" he said finally. "I mean, maybe you're telling me this as a big joke, a big laugh on me."

Mike's expression didn't change. "We're dead serious," he said. "And, yeah, we done something like this before."

"So what are we talking about?" Danny said, feeling a little excited and tough at the same time. He couldn't believe he was actually talking about a real theft. His palms were getting a little sweaty. "I mean, you got something in mind?"

"Warehouse, less than a mile from here," Wayne said. "Looks like a plain old brick building. Inside it's filled with jewelry, leather goods, electronics. All new. Easy to take out. Easy to sell."

"It's perfect," Mike said, looking around again. "We know how to get in, and how to get out. But we could use some help, if you got what it takes. We even got an old guy who'll buy it all from us. He's got connections. He gives us ten cents on the dollar."

"That's all?" Danny asked.

"It's the best you're gonna find," Wayne said. "That's it. You take him a piece of equipment worth two hundred bucks, he gives you twenty bucks. That's why we could use your help. We got to carry out a lot of stuff to make it worthwhile. There's an old abandoned garage a couple blocks away where we can stash it for a day or two until the old man is ready to buy it."

Danny paused a moment. His heart was pounding at the thought. Sure, it was risky, but it sounded more exciting than anything he'd ever done. Finally, he said, "I'm in," keeping a straight face as he said it. He didn't want to grin or act silly or show how excited he was.

"Talk to you later," Mike said, still eyeing Danny, still measuring him. "Like I said, from now on you don't talk to anybody. Not your parents, not your best friend, nobody. If you do . . ." He left it unfinished, but there was no mistaking the threat.

After they left, Danny sat down again in the grass. He couldn't believe what had just happened. His heart was still racing a little and his palms were still sweaty. A real heist. It was terrible to have to keep it to himself and not tell anyone, but he had no choice. Mike had made that clear.

❏ A couple of days later, the two boys walked up beside him as he was leaving school for home. "We'll show you the place," Wayne said as they continued to walk. Minutes later they were on a corner, staring at a nondescript building across the street. It was exactly as they'd said: plain, unremarkable, five stories high, with no sign of activity inside or out.

"It's quiet," Danny said finally.

"That's how we like it," Mike said, talking low. "Nice and empty, except for all that gear."

"Whose stuff is it inside?" Danny looked at Mike, then at Wayne.

"Who knows?" said Mike, still talking low. "Who cares?"

"You be here, on this corner, night after next, nine o'clock," Wayne said. "Make an excuse at home. Tell your parents you're at a friend's house or something. Just be here. If you don't show . . ."

Danny nodded. They didn't need to worry. There was no way he *wouldn't* show.

For the next two days, he could scarcely concentrate on even the simplest tasks. When his mother asked him to carry out the garbage, he began to carry out his schoolbook bag instead, until she stopped him and asked him where his mind was.

"I wasn't concentrating, I guess," he told her, startled by his own absentmindedness. All he could think of were his two new acquaintances, and how they were able to have two-hundred-dollar jackets and excitement when all his other friends seemed to be living such boring lives.

On the appointed evening, he told his parents he was going to a friend's house for a while. Outside, he sprinted as fast as he could run to the corner across from the warehouse. Once there, he leaned on a light post just outside a small, corner quick-stop market to wait for Mike and Wayne. He caught the scent of fresh vegetables from inside the market, and he could hear faint radio music coming from the back of the store.

Wayne and Mike startled him a little when they

walked up behind him at exactly nine o'clock. Neither said a word. Each was wearing a dark sweatshirt and running shoes. After glancing up and down the street a time or two, and checking to see that no one was watching them from inside the market, they motioned for him to follow. Danny was glad he had on his tennis shoes, although he hadn't thought about it when he'd gotten dressed that morning.

The brothers, with Danny following, walked casually across the street and strolled around to the side of the brick warehouse. Next to the building, separated by a high, chain-link fence, was a storage yard stacked with old pallets, boxes, and other shipping containers. No one seemed to be around the storage yard on the other side of the fence, and, in fact, there seemed to be no one in view from any direction.

Glancing around again, Mike stepped over to a ground-floor window in the building and smashed it in with his elbow. He knew exactly how to do it so he didn't get hurt. At the sound, all three boys froze, waiting to see if the noise attracted anyone. After several moments, Mike motioned to the other two. One by one they swung through the broken window and dropped a few feet to the cement floor below. Once inside, Mike and Wayne produced flashlights from under their shirts and began to pick their way around cases and cartons to the center of the building. Danny, following the other two, felt his heart jumping in double-time under his shirt.

He couldn't believe the sight that greeted them when they reached the center of the building and the other two boys moved their lights around. Stacked in neat piles, floor to ceiling, were hundreds, maybe thousands, of boxes of all sizes, with labels showing they contained everything from leather luggage to gold jewelry to electronic equipment. Maybe I could take a necklace or two home to my mom as a present, he thought. Then he remembered how crazy that would be. She'd go through the roof if she knew where it came from.

"You guys were right," he said, still shocked by the sight. "It's all here."

Mike put a hand over Danny's mouth, motioning for him to be quiet. In the shadows, out of the beam of the flashlight, Danny could see Mike and Wayne, cocking their heads, listening.

Already Danny was disgusted with himself. Here he was, blabbering away in the middle of a heist. He knew he still had a lot to learn. One thing was certain: these were the guys who could teach him. He strained, stock-still, listening, like the other two, for any telltale sounds that might spell trouble.

❑ Suddenly, Mike tensed and drew in his breath. For a moment, Danny heard nothing. Then it came to him, faint, yet menacing: footsteps moving slowly, almost casually, from a far corner of the building, toward them. They heard the crack! of a power switch and the entire first floor of the building was instantly bathed in a dusty yellow light.

"We've got to get out of here!" Wayne whispered while turning to search for possible escape routes. "Forget all this stuff! Let's just get *out*!" In a moment, both of Danny's companions had turned and were now sprinting away, through and around piles of cartons and boxes.

Fighting the urge to panic, Danny began to run as fast as he could in the general direction in which the brothers had gone. He tried to run while making as little noise as possible. He didn't want to call for help from Mike or Wayne, since that would tell whoever was coming exactly where he was. In moments he slammed into a huge wooden packing case he hadn't noticed in the shadows ahead of him, and turning from the case, he ran headlong into a steel beam that nearly knocked him unconscious.

"Mike! Wayne!" he called out, dragging himself to his feet and starting again in what he hoped was the right direction. No use trying to be quiet now, he thought. Everybody in the building must have heard him hit that carton. "Mike! Where are you guys?" Now his knee and elbow were hurting where he'd hit the beam and he was rapidly developing a hammering headache.

As he paused a moment to listen once more, he heard the same, steady approach of the footsteps. There was no other sound, not even the sounds of

Mike or Wayne running. They must have gotten out right away. Probably blocks away already. *Now what?*

His ears were playing tricks on him. Now the steps seemed to be coming from an entirely new direction. Suddenly he heard a new, and far more ominous sound: the menacing crackle of flames. In seconds, bright yellow-orange tongues of fire began to lick around the far walls and windows of the old building. He was drenched in sweat from a combination of fear and the growing heat.

Turning, trying to pinpoint the exact location of the approaching steps, he was grabbed by two slab-like hands and heaved into a swivel office chair. A rope was thrown over him, his arms were yanked tight to his sides, and he was swiftly tied to the chair. In the background, he could still hear the rumbling and crackling of the fire.

One of the hands grabbed the chair and spun it around, then stopped it, so that he was facing the person. In the shadows caused by the dim yellow light, he could just make out the head and neck of the person, who Danny could see was a large, older man.

When the man spoke, his voice was deep, ominous, and seemed to echo off the surrounding boxes. "You wanted in on a heist, huh? You wanted to be a robber?"

"I was just a little curious . . ." Danny began.

"Quiet!" the man snarled. "You're a young fool,

an idiot!" As he said this, he began to pace back and forth in front of Danny. "Do you know what it is to risk screwing up your life and getting a police record, all for a few bucks?"

"This is the first time . . ."

"I said *quiet*! Do you know what it is to risk your life for a few thrills? *Dumb*, that's what it is!" The man was pacing more and more, faster and faster, as he talked. "Do you know what robbers are? They're *stupid*! They're *always* stupid! And that means *you're* stupid, doesn't it?"

As the man said this, he turned and kicked Danny's chair so hard it fell over on its side with Danny still attached to it. His knee, elbow, and head hurt more than ever. "Look, we have to get out of here!" he groaned, struggling futilely to get out of the chair. "We'll burn to death!"

The man was still furious. "You wanted excitement? You got it!" He pulled several twenty-dollar bills from his pocket. "You want money so bad? Eat!" He knelt down and began to stuff the bills into Danny's mouth, until Danny was afraid he would suffocate. He began to gag and cough, spewing the bills from his mouth even as the man tried to feed him more of the foul-tasting paper. Retching on the floor, struggling not to choke, Danny wished more than anything that he had never let himself get involved in a heist, or be where this maniac could get at him.

The man stood up again and stared at Danny for

what seemed like several minutes. "You're a fool!" he rasped finally. "You risk your life to take what isn't yours? That makes you a fool, doesn't it?" Finally he untied the rope and pulled Danny to his feet. "Get out!" he half-shouted, pointing in the general direction of the window Mike had broken when they entered. "Learn from your mistakes!"

Danny hesitated, still trying to catch his breath, then turned and sprinted in the direction the man had pointed. The fire that so recently had licked and snarled around the building's walls appeared to have died down.

Fresh air never tasted so good, he thought, as he ran faster than he had ever run in his life, back toward his house. Around cars, through intersections, past parked cars, he ran, gulping air, his heart pounding, with no thought other than reaching the safety of his house and his parents and all the other things that were important to him. Rounding the corner near his house, he sprinted faster than ever. He slammed through the front door and sped up the stairs, not stopping until he had run into his room and flopped facedown on his bed.

❑ Over the next several days, although he did not see Mike or Wayne, he couldn't stop thinking about the bungled heist and the furious man. It made him shiver every time he thought about how close he'd come to disaster and possibly death. Several times, in chemistry class, during history, and even once during a physical education softball match, he was yelled at for not paying attention, and yet he couldn't tell the teachers or the coach the real reason for his absentmindedness.

After nearly a week, it was driving him crazy. He *had* to talk about it with someone. Mike and Wayne were gone, maybe dropped out of school, probably with good reason. They might have been in on other "heists." They might even have police records, for all he knew. It was probably a good idea that they were lying low. And yet here he was, keeping it all inside himself, feeling like he was going crazy.

"Tyler, you're my best friend." He tapped his fingers on the lunchroom table and fidgeted a little as a river of students passed back and forth in a nearby aisle and the noise of clanking dishes and voices swirled about their heads. He glanced around several times, but no one else seemed interested in what he was saying.

"Okay." Tyler, as usual, was smiling, relaxed, more apt to joke than take anything very seriously. "I'm your best friend. What are you trying to do? Propose?"

"I'm serious. I got to talk to somebody about something. You got to promise not to tell anybody."

"Okay. Shoot. What could be so important?"

"I got involved in a heist a few days ago. A robbery. Well, almost a robbery. Almost got caught. In fact, I almost burned up. I'm not kidding."

"You *what*?" Tyler wasn't smiling anymore. He

glanced about, then leaned closer, scowling at his friend. "Are you serious?"

As Danny told him about Mike and Wayne and the warehouse and the rest, Tyler leaned still closer, making certain no one else could hear. When Danny had finished, his friend said nothing for several moments, staring instead through the window across the lunchroom. Finally, he leaned back, looked around again, and half-whispered, "Show me this place."

"What for?"

"I'm just curious."

☐ After school, both boys called their parents and said they'd be a little late coming home, since they had to do a little "research."

"Not exactly a lie," Tyler said, hanging up the phone. "I'm glad they bought the story."

Walking in the direction of the warehouse, Danny's stomach began to feel a little queasy. "I'm not going closer than across the street," he said. "One visit inside that place was enough." In seconds, the little market where he'd waited before was in view. He pointed. "It's just across from that market."

"You sure this was it?" Tyler said when they reached the corner. For a moment, Danny couldn't speak. Where he had expected to see the warehouse, silent and foreboding, now stood a small, modern shopping plaza with several stores and a fast-food restaurant at one end.

"Wait a minute." Danny glanced around at the street, the little market and the street signs, and even peered up and down the block a couple of times before looking back at Tyler. "I know you think I've gone out of my head, but it *was* here . . ." he stammered. "I *know* it was. Wait here a minute." He walked into the little market, past trays and tables of fruit and vegetables, and motioned to an old man sorting fruit in the back. "Across the street, where the mini-shopping plaza is," he said. "What was there before?"

"Lousy little developments like that," the old man mumbled, continuing to sort fruit. "They bring traffic, noise, people throw trash . . ."

"Has it always been there?" Danny asked. He wondered if he was losing his mind.

"No, 'course not," the old man said, looking up at him. "It's been there a few years, I guess. Wait." Now the old man was thinking. "More than that. Maybe fifteen, sixteen years, I guess. Terrible things, those little shopping plaza things."

Danny's stomach was getting queasy again. "Do you know what was there before?"

"Of course. I been here more'n forty years. Before that plaza was there, it was just a big open lot for quite a while, after the truck dealer went out of business. Before that—now you're talking, oh, my, at least thirty, forty years—there was a building there. Brick, I think. A warehouse. Yeah, a warehouse, as

I remember. Maybe four, five stories high. Belonged to some store chain, but I don't remember who. Thing burned down right about the time I opened this market."

"Thanks," Danny mumbled, going back to his waiting friend.

"Thirty or forty *years*?" Tyler said, when Danny told him what the old man said. "Now I *am* interested. Let's swing by the library and check it out. They got old newspaper stories in the microfilm reader. It's like a mystery. You look for stuff on buildings, and I'll look up crime stories."

At a branch library two blocks from Danny's home, an older lady showed them where the microfilms were catalogued, and let them use a reader. Almost forty-five minutes later they'd found no photos or stories of the building.

"Gotta go," Tyler said finally. He leaned back in his chair and fiddled with the wheel on the reader. "My folks'll kill me as it is. I guess that old building never made the news."

"Yeah, I don't know." Danny idly spun the wheel on his machine, causing page after page of old newspapers from decades before to flick past on the screen. "I guess we'll have to give up." The whole thing was baffling. "I'm tired of staring at this stupid screen."

"Wait a minute." Tyler sat upright and peered at the screen in front of him. "Here's one. Let me see if there's an address here. Yeah! Bingo!" He turned and grinned. "Look here!"

Danny leaned closer to Tyler's machine. Highlighted on the screen was the front page of a newspaper from nearly forty years before. ". . . botched warehouse robbery," he began to read aloud. ". . . a bungled, tragic accident Tuesday in which a father and his two teenage sons were overcome by fumes from a faulty heating system while apparently attempting to steal merchandise from the building . . . emergency crews were unable to revive the three victims . . . firemen managed to remove the bodies before fire engulfed the structure . . ."

Tyler peered more closely at the photos accompanying the article. "Recognize anybody?" he whispered.

Danny nodded, too shocked to speak. Near photos of the burned-out warehouse were pictures of the three victims. The names were different, but there was no mistaking the faces: Mike, Wayne, and the older man in the building.

SOUVENIRS

Even before the trip had started, Becky had wondered why Jeff had to go along on the vacation. He was her cousin, of course, and it was just the two families going—her family and her Uncle Dan and Aunt Barbara—so it pretty much had to be. Just the same, he was an incredible pain in the neck. Even riding in the other car with his dad and mom, he was still not far enough away to suit her.

He was sixteen, not quite three years older than she was. But he acted like he was about twenty-two. He wouldn't be caught dead without his sunglasses, for example, and trendy clothes were the most important thing in the world to him. He didn't walk, he strutted. He didn't talk, he drawled. And he didn't sit, he sprawled. Everything in the entire known universe was boring, according to him, and he made it clear that riding across South Dakota to get to the Black Hills was about the last thing he ever actually *wanted* to do. He couldn't wait, he said more than once, to get to a city, or at least some kind of town with some "action." And he always made sure he treated Becky as though she were a hopeless child. He always gave her an exaggerated, toothy smile, because he knew it irritated her, and he called her stupid names like "acorn" and "gerbil."

"I wish he'd move to the South Pole or something," Becky had said when her dad first talked about the summer trip. "Why can't he just stay here at home? Chicago has plenty of action to suit a hotshot party animal like him."

"Oh, well," her dad and mom always said, "he *is* your cousin. If he's rude, just try and ignore him."

"I suppose," Becky always said, not meaning it.

On the other hand, she *was* excited at the prospect of seeing the famous Black Hills, especially Mount Rushmore with its mammoth carved-rock faces of presidents Washington, Lincoln, Jefferson, and Theodore Roosevelt—faces so realistic and so big they could be seen from sixty miles away. She was anxious as well to see the legendary Old West town of Deadwood, made famous by figures like Wild Bill Hickok and Calamity Jane.

When her dad had first curled open the highway map, before the trip, Becky had noticed that there was an awful lot of wide-open farmland and prairie to cross before they would skirt the north end of the Badlands and finally move into the pine-forested and mountainous Black Hills. She took along a few books, so that part of the trip wouldn't be quite so boring. At least there was one good thing: Jeff was planning to spend most of the trip in the other car with his parents.

❑ Now, a couple of days into the trip, she found herself gliding across a Dakota prairie so vast and flat she almost expected buffalo to come charging over the far horizon. It was beautiful, really, with the sweet scent of alfalfa blossoms lingering in the clear air and giant, cream-white clouds lolling in a brilliant azure sky. She had never seen country so open, so huge.

Sometimes, especially where the black earth had been turned up and crops were planted, she caught sight of tiny, striped animals that looked almost like chipmunks. Becky's dad, who had lived in this country when he was a boy, said some people called the animals "flickertails," but they were really just striped gophers. The curious little creatures had a way of standing bolt-upright whenever cars passed, like anxious little soldiers snapping to attention. Once in a while she caught sight of larger prairie dogs, rabbit-sized, black-tailed rodents running around mounds of packed dirt that Becky's dad said were the entrances to underground "villages." He said the prairie dogs, which Becky thought were cute, actually "barked" to each other whenever danger was near.

And every so often, they passed a farmer or rancher, his face burned to leather, guiding a large, gleaming machine of one kind or another under the merciless sun. She was sure Jeff wasn't even looking out of the car window to see the gophers or the farmers or anything else, for that matter. There was nothing here that he wanted.

One thing *she* wanted was a souvenir, something she could put on the shelf in her room back home. Maybe just a drink mug or a wall plaque or something to remind her later of the trip. Souvenirs always were fun. They let you live and enjoy vacations all over again, in a small way.

Marcy, her best friend back in Chicago, also had asked her to pick up "something western." Since the Black Hills were so close to Wyoming and the southern tip of Montana, she assumed everything even close was "western." Although that wasn't necessarily true, Becky assumed that finding a few western-style souvenirs wouldn't be much of a problem in this part of the country. If they didn't find any, she'd just have to have someone take her picture beside Wild Bill's grave and send *that* to Marcy.

Already, they had passed a few places that had SOUVENIRS stenciled on signs outside, but the places had looked sleazy, with almost nothing at all for sale. Becky knew that most such souvenir places were attached to gas stations or roadside restaurants. They were secondary operations, just something to keep passengers interested while the car was filled with gas.

"Imported junk," her father said, each time they

passed one of the tiny gas-station shops. "A few ash-trays, a few mugs, maybe a couple of postcards. I say we wait until we're actually in the Black Hills."

Becky hated to wait, but at this point there wasn't much choice. As they whisked past small towns along the Interstate, she scanned each side of the highway, hoping to spot a nice, big stand with lots of neat things for sale. She had all but given up when the car crested a gentle rise and she saw something up ahead, rising from the prairie like a city in miniature. SOUVENIRS/ GIFTS a giant sign shouted. The place looked nice and new, and it was not attached to a restaurant or gas station. Large side panels all around the structure were latched up and open, giving the stand an open-air look.

"Please, dad!" Becky pleaded. "This one looks nice. I just want something for Marcy and maybe something for me."

"I told you what I thought about those places," he said. Then he glanced at her in the rearview mirror and sighed. "Oh, well. Just be sure you don't take too long." He beeped his horn at Jeff's dad's car and they pulled off the Interstate. In seconds they opened their car doors to a blast of 90-degree heat rising off the asphalt parking lot. With the car's air condition-ing on, Becky had forgotten how hot it was outside. A few cars were parked nearby, and their occupants were browsing among the souvenirs.

As her eyes adjusted to the shade of the stand,

Becky couldn't believe what lay before her. Where the usual stand might have a few piles of cheap trinkets and maybe a few postcards, this one was incredible. Counter after counter held everything from beautiful polished rock pendants on leather thongs to crystal and blown-glass pieces to authentic Native American leather and beadwork, to arrowheads to samples of antique western barbed wire to tiny plastic vials containing actual samples of gold dust. Western clothes, beautiful Stetson hats and gleaming boots were on display in one area, while another contained framed oil-painted western scenes.

Even her parents were impressed. "Hard to know where to start," her dad muttered as he wandered off and began trying on cream-colored western hats in front of a mirror. Becky's mother already was absorbed in a collection of beautiful polished agates. A gentle breeze through the stand helped to temper the ferocious heat.

Jeff, as usual, made certain everyone knew he was bored with the stand and all that it held. "So, what's up, gerbil?" he drawled at Becky as she passed, flashing his toothy grin when she scowled at him. Ignoring the displays, he leaned on a post, adjusted his sunglasses, folded his arms and idly began watching traffic on the nearby highway. "I don't believe this heat," he groaned, to no one in particular. "I need a swim in a cool pool. As far away from here as I can get."

Heck with him, thought Becky. If he wants to watch cars, he can watch cars. She turned and began scanning the various counters, trying to decide what she'd like, and what she might get for Marcy.

The proprietors were a little different-looking, and definitely not the usual "have-a-nice-day" types. They both stayed near the cash register at the back of the stand, close to a doorway that appeared to lead to a small supply shed behind the stand. Both stared without expression at the customers as they drifted in and out. Maybe they don't speak English very well, thought Becky. The man was balding, and looked to be at least in his early sixties, if not older. He had a dark-gray, drooping mustache. The woman, who Becky assumed was his wife, was about his same age. She had a thin, hawkish face, and her dark hair was pulled back tight in a little knot at the back of her head. Both her dress and his shirt were of a bright, silklike material, more European than western in style.

Becky watched as another customer brought a small necklace to the couple. They took the money, placed the necklace in a bag, nodded and handed it to the customer without smiling. Not too friendly, thought Becky. Oh, well. Guess I wouldn't be, either, if I had to deal with strangers every day. She turned and began looking at several beautiful earthenware cups.

Next to the cups was a counter with a dozen or

more small perfectly carved figures, everything from cowboys, horses, and turtles to even a little Scotsman wearing a kilt. A cowboy figure would be great for Marcy to put on her desk at home, Becky thought, picking up one of the figures. When she saw the price on the bottom, she exhaled and quickly put it down again. "Forget it," she whispered to herself. "Marcy will have to settle for something that isn't so darned expensive." Near the figures were several silver bracelets, and they, too, cost more than she could afford.

An older car pulled up and parked, and Becky watched as an Indian man got out and began looking over some of the souvenir items. He was tall and muscular, with high cheekbones and a curved, chiseled nose. His shoulder-length, glossy-black hair was held in place with a colorful headband. On one of his wrists was a beaded bracelet, and he wore a tooled leather belt in his jeans that had the name BOB carved into the leather in the back. When her mother looked up, Becky smiled and nodded in the direction of the man. It wasn't every day she saw someone who looked like he must belong to a real Native American tribe. The man, who looked as if he was not in a very good mood, scowled as he picked up some of the Native American items on display.

She moved over to the counter containing the polished stone pendants, and found a few that weren't quite so expensive. The breeze sweeping through the stand from outside was warmer now and she was beginning to perspire a little. Looking through the pendants, she caught a slight movement at the corner of her eye. It was Jeff, motioning to his parents, signaling that he wanted to leave. He was clearly impatient now, and she could see that he was perspiring.

Finally, Jeff turned from his parents, threw his hands in the air and marched back to the old couple. Becky couldn't hear everything he said, but she did hear him say the words "water" and "soda" and "Coke." The old couple didn't seem to respond. Instead, the man slowly pointed toward the far side of the stand, where a narrow path led behind to the storage shed.

"Hey!" Jeff said suddenly, loud enough for everyone to hear. "You speak English?"

Becky was embarrassed by Jeff's rude behavior. She turned away, then looked again when she heard Jeff say, "You got a water fountain or a soda machine? You understand words like 'Coke' or 'Pepsi'? I'm dyin' of thirst!" The old man said something, too low to hear. "Okay, water, then. Anything wet."

Again the man pointed. Becky looked at her parents. She could tell they were uncomfortable, too. She looked back at the souvenirs, and tried not to look at the old couple. Actually, she wanted to find the water pump or a fountain, too, but she wasn't about to go out back right now. She didn't want the old couple to think she had anything to do with Jeff.

As she puttered about, looking for anything inexpensive, she noticed the moody-looking Indian man walk back to the couple and drop some sort of beaded necklace on the counter. He seemed even grumpier than before. Becky saw him hold the price tag up, near the old man's nose, then throw the necklace down again. As they talked, he wiped his forehead several times. The back of his shirt was wet, too, from perspiration. Finally he said something to the old man, and the man pointed toward the far side of the stand, just as he had for Jeff. The Indian turned and moved toward the outside path, shaking his head and mumbling as he went.

"Pick something so we can go," Becky's father said softly, nudging her a little. "I want to get going."

Finally she found a plastic drink mug with a photo of Mount Rushmore on it. It wasn't the greatest souvenir in the world, but it was one she could afford. She picked out a second one for Marcy and took them both to the old couple in the back. As she was counting out her money, her mom and dad and Jeff's parents brought a few things to the counter, too.

"Becky, you know where Jeff went?" her uncle Dan said, glancing casually around the store.

"Water fountain out back," she said, looking at the old man, whose expression never changed. "I'd like to grab a drink, too, before we get going." Dan and Barbara, and Becky's parents, too, seemed a little awkward around the old man and woman. Becky wondered how long it would be before Jeff finally learned some manners, especially around strangers.

When they had all paid for the items, Becky led the way to the path to get a drink of water before heading out on the road again. Actually, she would have preferred a soda, but at this point anything wet would be fine. The worn, dirt path ended behind the shed, part of which was hidden by one wall of the souvenir stand. There, attached to the rear outside wall of the shed, near a partly open door, they found a single, solitary water pipe with a rusty-looking tap. Hanging on the tap by a dingy cord was an old and well-used tin cup. The ground in a circle below the tap was spongy and wet.

"I guess I'd just as soon find some sodas up the road," Becky's father said, smiling at the others.

"Yuck!" Becky said. "I can wait, too." She made a sour face and turned to the others. "I wonder if Jeff drank out of this," she said. "How could any-body?"

"Guess it depends on how thirsty you are," her father said, still smiling. "But, as I said, I think I'll wait for a soda." He glanced about. "By the way, where is Jeff?"

"Probably out front," Becky said. "He's anxious to leave."

"No doubt," Dan said as he examined the tap. "This probably won't make anybody sick or anything," he said, straightening up and smiling, "but it isn't very appetizing. Let's go find Jeff and get going. There has to be a restaurant or something up the road."

At the front of the stand, where Jeff had waited for them before, there was no one. The only customers were an older couple, chatting as they tried on western hats.

"What the . . . ?" Now Dan was visibly irritated. "Where the heck did he go?" He turned to Jeff's mom and shrugged. "What's this? Another little trick? A way to punish us for stopping?"

Barbara touched his arm, as though trying to keep him calm, and said, "Let's just find him and go. No use having a fight over it."

"I'll look around back again," Becky said. "Maybe he went the other way around." She walked quickly, anxious to find Jeff and get into the air-conditioned comfort of the car. Passing the water tap, she met Dan coming around the other way.

"No where else to look," he said, now beginning to look worried. "I mean, where could he go? We're in the middle of nowhere." He wheeled about and walked into the stand, to the counter where the proprietors still stood. "My son, the young man with us—do you happen to know where he went?"

The couple merely stared, as before, and the old man shrugged.

Dan, now clearly irritated, stepped closer and

banged his fist on the counter. "Look," he said, his voice rising, "you must have seen him come back in. Where did he go?"

Still, the old couple merely shook their heads, and the old man raised his hands with the palms face-up, as though to say, "Beats me."

"This is ridiculous!" Dan half-shouted. "Okay, you don't know anything? Where's the nearest police station? How about a sheriff's station? The Highway Patrol?"

Becky's father stepped closer. "Look, Dan," he said quietly. "There's another possibility we didn't consider. He could have simply caught a ride with a passing trucker. Has he ever done anything like that? Has he ever run away?"

"Of course not!" Dan hissed, glaring at his brother. "That's crazy! Where would he run away *to*? We're in the middle of absolute *nowhere*!"

"Okay," Becky's father said, turning again to the old couple. "Where are the nearest police?"

The old man, still without any expression, pointed toward the highway. "Six, seven miles," he rasped, his voice sounding like a scraped steel drum. He turned and began to wait on the old couple, who had brought two hats to the counter.

"Follow me," Dan said to Becky's father. He walked quickly from the store, shaking his head in frustration.

"If Jeff simply took off, it's a dirty trick," Becky's

mother said as they followed Dan and Barbara's car out of the parking lot and back onto the highway. "I mean, what's he going to do? Does Jeff expect to just stand on the road up ahead, wave us down, and say it was all a joke? Some joke!"

❏ Suddenly, up ahead, Dan and Barbara's car exited the highway, made a U-turn and came to a stop. Dan trotted back to them. "Doesn't make sense," he said. "I don't remember any trucks going past. No cars, either, for that matter. I suppose they could have, but I don't remember hearing any. And besides, they would have had to stop, then start up again, and it seems to me we would have heard it."

Becky's dad scowled. "What other choice do we have?"

Dan thought a moment. "I'm going back to that stand," he said. "That rude old couple irritated me, anyway. They must have seen *something*. Maybe this time I'll pound it out of them."

"Just keep cool," Becky's dad called after Dan as he trotted back to his car. "It won't help if you start a brawl."

This time, Becky's dad seemed truly worried. "Dan's got a short fuse," he said as they headed back toward the stand. "If he starts a fight, we might see the police whether we want to or not."

Other tourist cars were in the parking lot this time, including the older car belonging to the Indian from before. Several families were moving casually among the displays on the counters. Becky wandered among them, trying not to be noticed. If Uncle Dan started a fight, she didn't want to be part of it.

Almost immediately, she heard Dan's voice rising as he questioned the old couple, and she heard her father's voice, more calm, obviously anxious to keep the situation under control. She continued to walk among the displays, trying to ignore the growing argument in the back of the store. She stole a quick glance, and saw that Dan was now waving his hands, while the old couple were as silent and unmoving as ever.

Becky smiled at a couple of the tourists, and browsed among the same items she'd looked at before. The blown-glass items were beautiful, and she especially liked the little figures that looked hand-carved. She wished she had a lot more money, so she wouldn't have to settle for plastic drink mugs.

Lingering a moment at the collection of small, exquisitely formed figures, her heart suddenly skipped a beat and she felt her blood turn icy cold. She opened her mouth to say something, but no sound came out. Among the tiny, costly statuettes of cowboys, horses, turtles, and other items were two new and perfect miniatures: one was the Indian man, complete with headband and a tiny belt with the name BOB in the back. The other was her cousin, Jeff, still wearing shades, his tiny face frozen in a permanent, cocky smile.

DRESSING UP

■ "Just think!" said Tom's friend, Larry, as he waved the newest edition of the school paper in the air. "Now that you've been voted school carnival king, you'll be able to date any girl you want! Girls love that kind of thing! And when you're meeting all these girls, be sure to introduce a few to me!"

"Give me a break," Tom mumbled as he sent the basketball in a high arc toward the basket above his garage door. "First of all, I didn't exactly ask to get elected, and second, I have to be king with Lisa Moore. She wanted to be queen. She's okay-looking, but I hardly know her. She's also a straight-A student. Probably she'll end up a professor at Yale."

"Well, that's not all bad."

"Sure, but what do we talk about? You figure she really cares how the Mets are doing this year?"

"Anyway, it's a chance to meet new girls. Not just Lisa. Your mom will probably want to take a lot of pictures. All the pictures will be of you lookin' sharp in your tuxedo." Larry laughed and stabbed one finger, as he always did, at the frame of his horn-rim glasses, pushing them up on his nose.

Tom made a gagging motion, scowling, then sank a hook shot from the free-throw line. "Monkey suit," he said, shaking his head. "Nothin' but a monkey suit. You look stupid in those things. I've seen guys at weddings in tuxes. They all look like stuffed sausages. The only guys who look good in 'em are millionaires and movie stars. And that sort of leaves me out."

"You never know," Larry said, still smiling. "Maybe you'll look so sharp, some movie company will come and insist you star in their next blockbuster. And then you can tell 'em, 'Look, guys, I got this friend, Larry, who's a great actor,' and then they'll hire both of us and we'll get rich. *Then* we'll look natural in tuxedoes, right?" He stabbed again at the glasses.

"Right." Tom dribbled from the outside, came up under the basket and did a reverse lay-up.

Larry grabbed the ball, walked to the free-throw line and dribbled it a few times. "Anyway," he said, cradling the ball for a moment, "a week from Friday is your big night. Better get to a tux rental place. Fame is waiting."

❏ "I think it's wonderful," Tom's mother said later, over dinner. "These are memories you'll have all of your life. Lisa Moore is a perfectly nice girl. You don't have to *marry* her, after all, or even date her if you don't want to. Someday you'll look back on this carnival king business and I think you'll be proud."

"Darn right!" Tom's dad chimed in. "We're going to take plenty of pictures, and I want you to get a fresh haircut, too."

"Aw, come on! Not a haircut! If I thought I had to go through all this, I would have told Mrs. Horowitz and her carnival committee that there was no way I'd be king. No way!"

"Don't be silly." Tom's mother patted him on the arm. "We're not asking you to join the Foreign Legion. Just a simple haircut. And I'd like you to go with me to look at tuxes tomorrow."

Tom's ten-year-old brother, Drew, grinned at him across the table. "How pretty you're going to look, Tommy," he mocked. "My big brother, Tommy Flash."

"Quiet, Drew." His father turned to Tom again. "Mom's right," he said, smiling. "We're not asking for the impossible. A little cooperation would be nice."

Tom stared at his plate for a moment, thinking. He didn't want a huge, knock-down-drag-out fight over this, especially with his parents. They were right. It wasn't a huge favor they were asking. On the other hand, it irritated him that this whole thing had more-or-less fallen on his head. He'd always gotten along fine with Mrs. Horowitz, the math teacher and carnival chairperson, and she seemed to like him, too. When she'd put his name into the carnival competition, he hadn't thought much about it. Now he was having second thoughts. A *lot* of second thoughts.

"Okay," he said slowly, still looking at his plate. "But if I'm doing you this favor, you can do me one, too. I don't want to have to go to some bigger place and spend a bunch of hours shopping for tuxes. There's a nice little tux shop next to the dry-cleaning place right here in Beamton. They must have something for rent that'll fit me."

"Well, I suppose," his mother said. "We'll see what they have." She sounded a little doubtful.

His mom, Tom knew, felt the same way others did in town. Although they lived only a couple of hours or so north of New York City, they sometimes became a little frustrated with the small community's limited selection in stores and services. On the other hand, Beamton was a safer and more peaceful place in which to live, which made some of the other frustrations more tolerable. Tom, for the most part, thought it was great living in a smaller community. It was easier to get on the basketball team, for example, and even if you got trapped into things like the school carnival, the people were generally pretty nice.

❑ The young guy in the tux shop the next day, when Tom and his mother walked in, was no exception.

He was relaxed and friendly, and even offered Tom a piece of hard candy from a jar on the counter. Tom guessed he was probably a college student.

"We carry a few styles by Pierre Cardin and Christian Dior," he said. "If you want, we can call other stores, and get you other styles by Raffinati, Lord West, and Perry Ellis . . ."

These names meant nothing to Tom. He stared absently at the mannequins, who looked about as bored as he was.

"What would you suggest for my son?" Tom's mother asked. "He's carnival king at his school."

Oh, brother, thought Tom. She even has to tell the guy in the tux shop.

Still, the guy was pretty nice. "Well," he said, sizing Tom up, "you're a pretty good-sized guy. My guess is you'll fit easily into a man's medium, say, around forty to forty-two."

"What style do you think?" Tom's mother asked, as she examined a couple of the mannequins. She turned to an open book on the counter. "This, maybe?" She pointed to a picture of a white one that had what Tom thought was a weird collar.

The clerk hesitated, glancing at Tom. "Tell you the truth," he said cheerily, pointing at a couple of different mannequins, "most young guys feel best in basic black Classic Notch styles, like these by Christian Dior and Pierre Cardin. They're quality tuxes, but they don't draw attention to themselves, the way some do."

Tom smiled his appreciation at the clerk. This guy definitely was all right.

Within minutes, Tom and his mother, with the clerk's help, had picked out a tuxedo, black tie, cummerbund/sash, matching pocket handkerchief, a pair of glistening, patent-leather shoes, and what the clerk called a "white-wing" shirt.

Next, Tom had to stand patiently while the young guy checked Tom's neck size, sleeve length, chest, waist, trouser length, height, and weight, to be certain the store had, or could obtain, the proper shirt and tux sizes to fit him properly.

"That should do it," the clerk said, still cheerful. "You know," he added, looking at his notes, "we've got one or two other customers who have just about exactly the same measurements as you do. They always rent the same tux models. Those guys are a little older, but still in shape. You must play sports."

"Well," Tom mumbled, "some basketball, baseball, a little football, soccer . . ."

"I guess you play sports," the clerk laughed. He turned to Tom's mother. "You can pick this up the day before the carnival, and at that time, we'll have this guy try everything on to make sure it's okay. That way, if something's wrong, we've got time to replace it. Then just bring it all back the day after the carnival. That's all there is to it."

❏ "I was impressed," Tom's mother said, on the way home. "I think you're going to look pretty good."

Jury's still out on that one, thought Tom. I'll decide after the try-on.

A little over a week later, they were in the shop again. This time, Tom's father and Drew went along. When Tom came out from the dressing room, Drew whistled.

"You look fantastic," his mother said, smiling.

Tom's dad nodded. "You sure do, son. You sure do."

Looking in the three-way mirror, even Tom himself had to smile at the image. He *did* look pretty sharp, he had to admit. In fact, this was about the best he'd ever looked. Of course, he wouldn't admit it to Larry, and certainly not to Drew.

❏ The next day, Larry was on the phone before Tom even got up. "Big night tonight," Larry said, and whistled. "Remember what I said. Any extra girls you meet, toss 'em my way."

Tom stumbled down to breakfast, and less than an hour later, he was sitting in a barber chair while a stylist fussed over his hair. "Just not too short," is all he could say. "I hate it when it's too short."

By midafternoon, he was secretly a little anxious to slip on the tux and see how he looked with the new haircut. He took a long, hot shower, used some of his dad's expensive cologne, brushed his hair the way the stylist had, and walked downstairs for pictures. Even Drew didn't crack a joke. It was a good sign. Apparently he looked all right.

The way his mom and dad fussed around, getting this pose and that one in the front yard, the neighbors must have thought he was getting married or something. He was relieved when it was time to get in the car and head for the school gymnasium.

❑ A crowd already had gathered when they arrived in the school parking lot. Several of his friends, and some of his teachers, waved and smiled as he stepped from the car. The school carnival had been going on for hours already, with food booths, games of skill, a "dunk-the-teacher" ball-throwing contest, and a slam-dunk basketball contest with a five-dollar prize.

Leaving his parents, Tom wandered around the gym for a few moments, looking for people he knew. He stopped by an open area where band members were setting up music stands, and the music teacher, Ms. Lamont, was arranging sheet music on the piano.

A moment or so later, a couple of teachers spotted Tom and hustled him off to a room near the gym to wait for the grand finale and the entrance music, which would be a signal to him and Lisa. She was already in the room, waiting and nervous-looking, when he stepped in.

She smiled, made a little small talk, and checked her dress and corsage repeatedly while they waited. She was quite pretty, really, with her light-brown hair tumbling stylishly about her slim neck and shoulders. She seemed nice, too. Maybe I judged too quickly, Tom thought, as she checked her dress one more time.

"I guess all we have to do is walk in, stand on stage for a few minutes while the principal says a few words, then cut out," Tom said, smiling.

"Hope that's all there is to it." She exhaled and readjusted her corsage slightly. "You look nice," she added.

"You, too." He shifted his weight from one foot to the other, and checked his watch. "Nice dress."

When they started the music, Tom felt a quick bolt of nervousness, then it dissolved as he and Lisa walked up the long open space in the gymnasium between waving crowds of people. Larry was there, near the front, giving him the thumbs-up sign, and so were his parents. It seemed only seconds, with a few words from the principal, Mr. Danvers, and Mrs. Horowitz, before someone put crowns on their heads. Then, as Tom's mother and other parents popped dozens of camera flashes, they headed out again, through the same crowd. Tom dropped his spray-painted crown on a table near a door on the way out.

Outside, people milled about, eating cookies and drinking punch, while others sat and visited at long tables covered with white paper. Tom's parents were still inside, chatting with a couple of neighbors. Lisa squeezed Tom's hand, then drifted away with several of her girlfriends.

"Good job!" Larry was still grinning as he clapped

Tom on the back. "Mr. Majesty, himself." He turned for a moment, grabbed four cookies off a plate and tossed one to Tom. "So. Want to find some girls?"

"I don't know. I guess." Tom put the cookie down without eating it. An odd, strange feeling had been growing inside him since he got here, one he'd never felt before.

"You all right?" Larry stared at him, and then at the cookie. "You look like something isn't quite right."

"Oh, really?" Tom stared at his friend without smiling, then moved to a nearby table, where someone had left a half-full pack of cigarettes. He took one out, stuck it in his mouth and began looking about for a lighter.

"Are you *crazy*?" Larry hissed, stepping in front of Tom. "You don't even smoke! I wouldn't even joke like that. Coach sees it, and you can kiss away your spot on the basketball team."

"Joke?" Tom's voice was lower now, ragged-sounding, and his eyes had narrowed. "Get out of my way. I need to find a light." He scanned several nearby tables, looking for a spare match or a lighter. Finally he gave up and tossed the cigarette to the ground. Grabbing an empty cup, he walked to a coffee urn, filled the cup, and walked back toward Larry while sipping from the cup.

"You don't drink coffee, either!" Larry said, scowling. "Are you out of your mind?"

Slowly, deliberately, his face still a stony mask, Tom set the coffee cup on the table, stepped closer to Larry, grabbed him by the shirt-front and slammed him against the outside of the gymnasium with such force it knocked his glasses into the nearby grass.

Larry opened his mouth to speak, but said nothing. His eyes were wide open in a look of complete surprise.

"Butt out!" Tom snarled. "What I do is *my* business!" His voice was a rasping growl, and he had all he could do to contain the strange, boiling anger welling up inside him.

When he let go, Larry rearranged his shirt, stepped over to pick up his glasses, and walked away, shaking his head, without saying a word. Tom, the odd, gnawing anger still eating through him, began to pace a little, near the tables, punching, over and over, one fist into his other hand.

"Tom? Are you all right?" This time the voice was Lisa's. She reached out to touch his arm, then thought better of it and pulled her hand back. "You look like something's wrong."

"Take a hike!" Tom snarled without slowing his pace. "I don't feel like talking."

Lisa exhaled, throwing her hands up in frustration, then turned and walked away. Within minutes she was back, this time with Larry. "Will you tell us?" she said. "We're your friends. At least, Larry's your friend, and I'd like to be."

"Don't crowd me," Tom snarled and turned from them to walk, alone, among the tables.

❑ "Ready to go home, dear?" It was Tom's mother's voice. They were walking from the gymnasium, foam coffee cups in hand. "You look so terribly handsome, we'll have to take another picture or two when we get home before you take off the tuxedo."

Tom remained silent as they walked toward the parking lot. Halfway to the car, they heard running steps and turned to see Mr. Kiley, the assistant principal, hurrying to overtake them.

"I'm sorry," he said, puffing, "but there was a slight oversight, and we needed to catch you and let you know of it before you got away." He cleared his throat, and turned to Tom. "It seems Ms. Lamont took her watch off and laid it on the piano while she prepared her music and got the band members situated before the procession in the gymnasium." He seemed to be picking his words carefully, so as not to offend Tom or his parents.

"Yes . . . ?" Tom's mother said.

"Well," Mr. Kiley said, "apparently one of the band members saw Tom put the watch in his pocket." He looked a little embarrassed, and still seemed to be picking his words very carefully. "With all the noise and activity, I'm . . . certain he was just holding it for safekeeping for Ms. Lamont . . ."

"Tom . . . ?" His father and mother both turned

to him. He shrugged, reached into a pocket of the tux and handed the watch to Mr. Kiley, who seemed very relieved.

"I don't understand," Tom's father said on the way home. "You have a watch in your pocket, and you don't even remember taking it?"

"Leave me alone," Tom mumbled, staring from the car window. "Just leave me alone." He couldn't wait to get out of the tux and into his old jeans.

❏ "Larry's here," Tom's mother said the next morning, leaning into the door of his room, as Tom rolled over, opened sleep-heavy eyes and tried to focus. "It's almost noon. Go talk to him." Her voice was cool, detached, and she wasn't smiling.

Larry looked a little nervous as Tom trudged to the front door and stared through the screen. "You acted pretty weird yesterday at the school," he said. "I never saw you act that way before. Thought I'd just swing by and see how things were going. You seemed really mad at me, or at somebody."

"I'm not mad at you. Truth is, I don't remember much about it," Tom mumbled, squinting in the light. "Glad it's over. I don't want to get dressed up like that again for a long time."

Larry seemed more relaxed now. "Yeah, well, it's over. Maybe we can shoot a few baskets later."

Tom nodded. "Stop around this afternoon. We'll shoot a few."

"We'll return the tux right after lunch," Tom's mother said, setting down a plate containing a tuna sandwich and a little pile of potato chips. "You weren't very nice yesterday."

He shrugged. "I don't know. I feel fine now."

Before they entered the tux shop, Tom saw through the window that the same clerk was on duty. Carrying the tux into the store, he felt a curious force, an almost ominous energy, rising from the garment and into his hands.

"Don't wrinkle it," his mother cautioned, as Tom laid the tux on the counter. Without realizing it, he'd held in it such a tight grip his fingers were white.

The clerk was as friendly as before, and tossed Tom another piece of hard candy. "Glad you were so prompt in bringing it back," he said. "We have another customer who's almost exactly your size, and likes the same style tux. The one he usually takes is getting a little hole repaired in one sleeve. We don't have a big selection in each style, so it'll be easy to have this one dry-cleaned, pressed up nice, and ready for him."

"I'm curious," Tom's mother said, making polite conversation. "What kind of people tend to like what kind of tux styles?"

The clerk laughed. "Varies all over the place. Of course, in a little shop like this, there isn't much choice. We have to keep dry-cleaning the ones we have and renting them out again. But it varies. For example, the guy that will be taking your son's tux is a real great guy, a retired English professor at the community college right here in town. A real gentleman. Reminds me of my grandpa. Rents from us every so often."

"The same tux?" Tom asked.

"Same tux. Our stock's pretty small, like I said. This time I'll give him the one you wore. And I'll tell you one better than that." He grinned and spoke a little lower, glancing about to be certain no other customers were in the store. "Before you rented this one, I rented it—the very same tux—several times to Joe Tambler. It was his favorite, before he had me order him a new one of his very own, just like it."

"Who's Joe Tambler?" Tom's mother asked.

"Well, I suppose it's not for me to say," the clerk said, although he clearly enjoyed telling it. "Some people say he's a big-time gangster. He comes up here from the city when he wants to get away for one reason or another. Anyway, I guess he's got a terrible temper. And he supposedly killed some people, too. I don't know, though. He was always okay to me and gave me big tips. I haven't seen him around for a while. Maybe he spends more time in the city now."

All the way home, Tom couldn't stop thinking about the tux. As soon as he was in the house, he called Larry. "Can you believe I was wearing the same tux some big-time gangster wore? The same tux!"

133

Larry rolled the thought around in his head for a moment before he spoke. "You know what's kind of spooky?" he said finally. "What if Tambler, you know, *killed somebody* while wearing *that tux* . . . Is that a weird thought, or what?"

"I don't want to think about it," Tom said. "I really don't."

❏ "Terrible thing," Tom's dad said two days later as he glanced over the front page of the paper during breakfast. "Absolutely senseless."

"What's that?" Tom's mother asked.

"There was a shooting last night at the country club, right here in Beamton. The shooter was a retired English professor, of all things, who used to teach at the community college. Can you believe that? It says the guy apparently became enraged at a remark another party-goer made. The old guy grabbed a gun from a security guard and began firing. Killed one person and wounded two others. People who were there, people who know this guy, said he's normally a kind and gentle man. They can't figure out why he'd act that way."

"Wait a minute," Tom said, glancing at his mother.

She lowered her coffee cup slowly and stared at the paper. "Did you say English professor?" she said, and looked at Tom.

"Right there it is," Tom's dad said. "Front page."

He reached over and laid the folded newspaper between Tom and his mother. Below a large headline about the killing was a photo showing officers taking a distinguished-looking, gray-haired man in handcuffs toward a waiting police car. In the photo, the dazed, confused-looking man was wearing a tuxedo that looked exactly like the one Tom had rented for the school carnival.